28 Days of Neon

Meira Rosenberg

ALL THINGS
THAT MATTER
PRESS

Thank you so much to my readers, critique groups, and friends, with special thanks to Barbara Gold, Connie Jordan Green, Joe and Faith, Lily Hope, and All Things That Matter Press for going above and beyond.

For my extraordinary parents, whom I miss every day, and for the square pegs, who make the world a more interesting place.

And to David, my love and best friend, and to our children and the kiddo, with so much love.

CHAPTER ONE

Wednesday Morning, 7:00 a.m.

I cross and uncross my legs, jiggle my right foot, and think. Again. And again. If I were a cartoon, and there was one of those cartoon bubbles above my head, it would look like this:

Empty. Blank. Nothing, Nothing, Nothing.

I could fill that cartoon bubble if this were pre-algebra or social studies. But this looking deep into my soul, introspective-type stuff isn't working for me. Except it has to. Because I have to get a Miracle before the 2,419,200 seconds I have left tick-tock tick-tock all the way to nothingness.

2,419,200 seconds.

　　　　　Tick

40,320 minutes.

　　　　　Tock

672 hours.

　　　　　Tick

28 days.

　　　　　Tock

I have twenty-eight days left to live.

Which is why I'm counting by seconds.

And why it makes me more than a little bit anxious to realize that in the ten minutes I took to write this, I'm down by 600.

2,418,600 seconds.

Left　To　Live

Flashback, Fifteen Minutes Earlier

I'm walking past Mom and Dad's bedroom before school when I hear, "I thought we decided not to tell Neon, not to ruin her last four weeks."

Last four weeks? Are we moving or something?

I stop short and slide my feet flat across the nubby mocha carpet so I can slink closer without making a sound. Rainbow pads silently beside me, her thick black fur shedding against my red flannel pajama pants.

We press our ears against the door. Rainbow's floppy ears point straight up in listening mode.

"She's only twelve." Mom's voice catches, then breaks.

Like she's ... crying?

"Honey, Dr. shizezzl zzetzzet said 'zzetzzetzze ...,'" Dad begins.

What doctor? I press my ear harder against the door.

"... and focus on making her comfortable," he finishes.

Comfortable? Since when do my parents worry about making me comfortable? We already have the best La-Z-Boy loveseat recliner in town.

"... can't ... four weeks ... only twenty-eight days ... I never thought ..."

No doubt about it. Mom is crying. Definitely crying.

"... we'd lose her so soon."

Rainbow's tail thumps the wall.

"Neon?" Dad calls. "Is that you out there?"

I lift my index finger to my lips and pat Rainbow on the rump so she'll follow me down the hall to my room. I walk inside to get dressed for school then sit on the crumpled lavender quilt on my unmade bed instead to figure out what my parents were talking about.

But their words are a mixed-up jumble crashing inside my brain.

Four weeks   *ONLY TWELVE*   **LOSE HER LOSE HER LOSE HER**

Make her comfortable   Four weeks

NOT TELL   *ONLY TWELVE*

DOCTOR   *Make her* comfortable

Twenty-eight days

Until they're not.

Breakfast, Thirty Minutes Later—As In Now

I am gulping down my first spoonful of whole grain, organic Oatie-Oats topped with milk squeezed from Holy Cows and blueberries of pure unpesticided joy as Rainbow wanders into the kitchen. She plops her furry self on the wood floor across my freezing feet. I snuggle my toes under my living, breathing foot warmer.

"Well, Neon," Dad looks up from the morning news on his iPhone and says, "what's on the agenda at school these days?"

Then he smiles.

I spit out half my mouthful of cereal as the Goddesses of All Things Organic quiver in shock. Dad never talks at breakfast until his second-and-a-half cup of coffee, unless he's thinking out loud about amps or circuit breakers or other electrician stuff.

And I have never seen him smile, coffee or no coffee, before 7:23 a.m.

Never.

Whatever the doctor told my parents, it must be worse than I thought.

Scratch that.

Twenty-eight days to live is as bad as it gets.

I try to smile back at Dad, but a happy, smiley feeling is not exactly the emotion I'm having right now.

I don't get it. Why isn't Dad looking at me with his Protect-You-from-the-World eyes and telling the truth in his Gentlest-Dad-in-the-Galaxy voice?

I look down at the pine kitchen table and focus on the swirly brown knot next to my cereal bowl to hide the fire-hot tears burning my eyes, but the fireworks burning through my brain are exploding. I try to figure out what to say without giving away the fact that I was eavesdropping.

Hang on.

Dad's not about to go apoplectic over my eavesdropping when I only have twenty-eight days left to live. Is he?

"Dad?" I begin.

Then my Oatie-Oats plummet to the pit of my stomach.

If I ask—if Dad answers ...

I'm not ready.

I'm not ready to hear it.

From Dad.

For real.

"So?" Dad puts down his phone. "What's new in Seventh Grade Land?" He rests his chin in his hand, aims his green eyes at me, and waits.

"Not much," I finally say.

"Give me one," he says, using his trademark technique for getting around a nothing-type answer as Mom comes into the kitchen.

"In Life Skills yesterday, Ms. Frasier said, 'You're as ready as you'll ever be for eighth grade. My job is done.' Then we watched *Pirates of the Caribbean* five. The other teachers scored *Pirates* one, two, three, and four from the library media center before Ms. Frasier could get them."

"Sounds fine to me. You'll be working hard enough in eighth grade." Dad smiles again, sending shudders of shock through my nervous system. "It's a whole new ballgame."

"Just enjoy it, Sweetheart." Mom walks behind my chair, smooths my light brown hair, and wraps her arms around my shoulders. "It's not every day you can goof off in school."

They're good. Really good. Mom doesn't even tear up as she hugs me.

Who knew my parents were such good liars?

Life Skills, My View

Never drink alcohol. Never take drugs. Do not hold hands with boys until you are forty.

Life Skills class was supposed to get us ready for infinity and beyond, aka eighth grade, high school, and happily forever after.

It used to be coed until a few nosy parents complained about the girls and boys being together while learning about ... whisper whisper whisper SHHHHHHH ... so now they divide us for all the juicy important stuff. Which turned out to be everything. Which pretty much tanked the whole point of Life Skills.

It would have been a lot more useful to keep the boys with us. That way, when Eddie Rasmussen snapped my bra when we were standing in the hall before class last week and said I have great knockers—

Hang on. Two points here. First off, what twelve-year-old says *knockers*? And secondly, considering that I'm still wearing a training bra, my knockers aren't exactly doing any knocking.

Anyway, when Eddie did that, Ms. Frasier would have seen that the only rational response was to punch him. How was I supposed to know he'd had a root canal that morning?

The principal, Ms. Goodworthy, said I should have reported him for sexual harassment. She said Eddie had no right to do or say that stuff because my body is private and Eddie has to learn appropriate behavior.

My point exactly.

I just figured a punch in the jaw was a good way to teach him.

Which goes back to my question. What use is Life Skills if all we've learned is how to deal with other twelve-year-old girls, who, by the way, will not be twelve for much longer? If Ms. Frasier doesn't see the jerkface boys in action, how will she know to teach us when to punch them in the jaw and when to tell the principal?

I've known Eddie Rasmussen ever since we were in Toddler Tempos and Tunes together. He was a jerkface at two and he's a jerkface at twelve. He bullies everyone—girl, boy, or twelve-week-old puppy. Eddie Rasmussen has always been an equal opportunity jerkface, and if Life Skills isn't going to teach the rest of us how to deal with a jerkface like him, then,

Life Skills = No Skills = One Big Fat Waste of Time.

CHAPTER TWO

Living Room, 7:30 a.m.
(2,417,400 seconds left to live)

I'm scooching under the sofa in the living room to search for my sneakers when Rainbow barks. I scooch back out and follow her gaze to the photos on top of the ancient baby grand piano we inherited from Grandma.

I raise my eyebrows at Rainbow. She barks again. Then she points her nose toward the photo of my seven-year-old brother Jonathan—aka J.B., aka the Dweeb—sitting on the wooden steps to our cabin at the lake.

And I see it.

A Daddy Long-Legs doing an eight-legged Tango across the bay window behind the piano.

Everyone says that Daddy Long-Legs don't bite. And that they're not real spiders.

I don't buy it.

Besides, I have the inside-outside rule for bugs.

Inside, it's Bye-Bye Bugsy. Outside, I, Neon the Benevolent, grant those creepy-crawlers a reprieve.

But we're inside now, and it's doomsday time.

I roll up a magazine and hold it in the air. Swinging my arm back, I'm ready to smash the alleged non-spider to oblivion.

My elbow freezes in mid-pivot.

Rainbow tilts her head and wags her tail. She knows the drill, and I'm not following it. I unroll the magazine and edge it inch by inch to the Daddy Long-Legs who tip toe tip toe tip toe tip toe tip toe tip toe tip toe tip toes onto the glossy cover. I cup my hand over it, and before it can bite me, Rainbow and I race out the door to the daffodils in the front garden. Then I set it free.

I hold Rainbow's collar so she doesn't chase after that Daddy Long-Legs and scarf it down.

We watch it skitter away, and I feel kind of relieved.

The idea of smushing that alleged non-spider to smithereens was giving me a sick feeling right in the fist of my stomach.

Now that I have my own date with oblivion.

My Bedroom, A Few Minutes Later

I uncrumple my lavender quilt, climb on my bed, and fluff my purple patchwork pillow. I open my nightstand drawer to take out my diary again and prop it against my knees. Then I lean back and begin to write.

Dear Smush,

This morning I saved a life. It was only a Daddy Long-Legs' life, but it felt pretty okay to watch it scoot away instead of cleaning its squished guts off our bay window.

I just Googled it, and they really don't bite. At least, not the ones around here.

I could make Daddy Long-Legs the exception to my inside-outside rule.

Unless one is crawling up the wall while I'm on the toilet.

I close my diary, hop off my bed, and—

I know what I'm going to do.

Just like that.

Maybe that's how it works with this deep, introspective thinking stuff. You wait it out, then:

BOOM! FLASHING LIGHTS! APPLAUSE! CHEERS!

Your subconscious mind gives you the answer.

I know how I'll get a Miracle. How I'll try, anyway.

I'm going to do a good deed every single day.

I know. It's not a perfect answer. I'm not what you'd call naturally helpful. Or unusually kind.

But my subconscious mind doesn't have a lot of practice at this sort of thing, and it's not like I have days and days to spare while I wait to see if it comes up with anything better.

I sit down at my desk, open my diary, and write on top of a blank page,

28 Days of Good Deeds

Then I think about that Daddy Long-Legs, cross out the 28, and write,

27 Days of Good Deeds

1.	10.	19.
2.	11.	20.
3.	12.	21.
4.	13.	22.
5.	14.	23.
6.	15.	24.
7.	16.	25.
8.	17.	26.
9.	18.	27.

I tuck my left leg under my tush. I jiggle my right foot.

I switch and tuck my right leg under my tush. I jiggle my left foot.

I try to imagine what my best friend Genna would do.

Genna would know a bazillion good deeds to do without even thinking.

I, on the other hand, do not sense one single other idea for a good deed bubbling up from the innermost depths of my mind.

:(

I sigh and stare at the twenty-seven blank spaces on my list. Then I rip out the page and write all over again.

Good Deed #1. Saved a Life.

Maybe it was only an alleged non-spider. But it's a start.

"Neon," calls Dad. "You're going to be late."

I leap out of my chair and shove Smush into my nightstand drawer. Then I tear through my closet to find my old sneakers and grab my backpack.

Time to pretend that everything's just fine.

Mrs. Valentine, On The Way To School
"Neon? Hel-looow?"

I look down to see Mrs. Valentine kneeling beside her white picket fence that's covered with pink climbing roses all summer long. Gray curls peek out from under the crimson and navy Huskies cap she only wears when she's working in the garden.

"Sorry." I hurry toward her. "I didn't hear you."

She stands and walks to meet me, a thin line of dirt trailing behind from the clump of dandelions in her hand as she opens the front gate. "Lost in thought? Social studies or math?"

"Huh?" I ask, still not quite listening.

"Big test today?"

"Oh." I pause. Compared to the thoughts I was having just now, a big test would be pure joy. "Nope." I shake my head. "Not today."

Not that kind of test, anyway.

"Must be the weather. These lovely spring days make it hard for a body to concentrate." She coughs and covers her mouth with the back of her dandelion-filled hand.

"Are you okay?" I ask.

She waves her other hand. "Allergies. All this pollen in the air."

"You sure you're okay?" I ask as she coughs again.

"Absolutely." Mrs. Valentine nods. "You'd better get going so you're not late. I'll see you tomorrow." Her gray eyes crinkle as she smiles. "As usual!"

Tomorrow is Thursday. Every other Thursday, we don't have after-school activities, and before I go home, I stop next door to visit Mrs. Valentine.

She comes to my house, and my family visits her lots of other times, too, but every other Thursday is just for us. It's our usual.

"Tomorrow," I call as I turn down the street. "For sure."

Homeroom, Wilson-Pike Middle School, 8:10 a.m.
(2,415,000 seconds left to live)

"You're late," Genna whispers as I slip quietly into my seat.

Genna and I have been best friends since the birth of our universe, as in, before either of us can remember. She's the nicest girl in the seventh grade and the prettiest, too, with her warm brown skin and curly black hair. But it's her eyes that clinch it. People get so lost in Genna's liquid brown eyes, they fall right in and can't climb out.

"Neez?"

"Hmmm?" I say.

"Why were you—"

"Tommy!" Ms. Redmond is standing in front of his desk, holding her hand out. "Cell phone."

"The bell didn't ring yet," Tommy complains with a scowl.

"It rang five minutes ago, which you would have realized if you were engaged with actual human beings instead of letting that brain-numbing device devour your brain cells one-by-one."

I'm almost never late, but whenever anyone is, Ms. Redmond doesn't notice. She's oblivious to the rest of us because Tommy sucks up all her attention in their daily duel over his phone.

Every. Single. Morning.

On the one hand, he's a major pain. On the other hand, since the rest of us can do pretty much whatever we want, I don't totally hate Tommy Hillandale for being endlessly annoying.

I take my binder out of my backpack to see if I forgot my math homework again.

"So," asks Genna, "why were you late?"

"Overslept," I say, leafing through my assignments.

Genna stares at me with her liquid brown eyes. "But you never—"

"Last chance, Tommy," Ms. Redmond says.

Tommy plops his phone into Ms. Redmond's still outstretched hand and makes a face as she walks to the front of the room.

"And wipe away that nasty smirk, please," Ms. Redmond says, without even turning around to look.

"Neez." Genna frowns. "Are you sure everything's okay?"

The bell rings before I have to think of an answer.

And before Genna's supercharged, whiz kid brain figures out how not okay everything really is.

Lunch, Wilson-Pike Middle School Cafeteria, 11:55 a.m.
(2,401,500 seconds left to live)

All morning since homeroom, I haven't been able to focus. Not in English, or Science, or Life Skills. My parents' words are stuck inside the centrifuge in my brain, spinning faster and faster, then breaking apart. But no matter how many different ways I put them back together, there's no unhearing something once you've heard it.

"Ahhhhhheeeeeee!" Smack! Casey trips and crashes his tray right into me.

"Ow!" I clutch my stomach.

Casey's Gatorade bottle flips through the air. Its ice-cold contents flood his tray, splash over Angel Sills' white cotton cardigan, and spill in neon blue cascades to the dingy gray floor.

Ms. Petrie, Wilson-Pike's very tall, very skinny special education teacher, jumps up from the table to get help. She pauses with a worried look at the three kids left sitting at the table, like she doesn't want to leave them on their own, and turns to me.

"Are you hurt?"

I shake my head. "I'm okay. I'll get the custodian."

Ms. Petrie's mouth gapes open like I'm a rhinoceros with wings as I take off. I grab a stack of napkins on the way, then push through a line so long you'd think we were at Dairy Queen on the Fourth of July.

One minute later, I'm back with Mr. Sebastian and his mop, but we're about fifty-nine seconds too late. Ms. Petrie is helping Angel up. She must have slipped on the Gatorade because her jeans are stained neon blue now, too.

"I ruin Angel. Angel blue." Casey's big, gloppy tears pour down his red cheeks, boogers cover his nose and mouth, and he's running his hands through his blond hair, streaking it blue. All in all, not his best look.

Angel wraps her arms around her chest and stands statue still, except for the shivering. It doesn't take a Gatorade tsunami to freeze in this always freezing cafeteria, but it sure can't help. She's

12

gotta feel pretty yucky.

"Neon," Genna calls from the dirty dish conveyor belt. "Is everything okay?" She squints to see what's going on.

I raise my index finger to give Genna the one-second sign, and hand the napkins to Ms. Petrie.

Then I look at Angel, whose hazel eyes pool with tears. Her red hair is fixed in two perfect pigtails, a hot pink butterfly barrette clipped above each one. Under her formerly white cardigan, she's wearing a crisp formerly white blouse, and her blue jeans still have a crease down the middle. A perfect crease, the kind that can only be created with heavy starch and an iron.

I never looked at Angel before—not the way I look at kids who aren't in special ed. Even when I see them in English or art or another of my classes, I always think of Angel and Casey and the other special ed kids as this blob of Special Eddies whom I rush past in the hall.

If I ever think about them at all.

I never noticed how nicely Angel's clothes match or how those barrettes match her hot pink watch.

I never noticed that somebody loves Angel.

A lot.

"Here." I take off my pink sweatshirt, hold it out to her, and smile. "It matches your barrettes."

She stares at the sweatshirt but doesn't move. I reach and begin gently lifting her neon blue soaked cardigan off her wet shoulder.

"No! No! No, no, no!" She shakes her head as her shouts get louder and louder.

Mr. Sebastian pats her shoulder, but she keeps shouting.

I don't know what to do. My stomach muscles tighten. The bruise swelling around my bellybutton pulses and pounds.

Ms. Petrie looks from Casey and the pile of Gatorade, tears, and booger-soaked napkins in her hand to me.

"For Angel." I toss the sweatshirt to her. "She's cold."

"Neon," Ms. Petrie calls as I rush away. "Thank you. That was actually very ... thoughtful." Her voice rises with a note of surprise.

I give a quick nod. As I walk across the cafeteria as fast as I can to meet Genna, I realize I've never once wondered. Who will take care of Angel when she's all grown up?

Then it hits me, as hard as Casey's tray all over again. Except this time, it's crashing inside my brain.

Angel, at least, gets to grow up.

Neon Blue, As In My Name—Not Gatorade

My mom had a hippie phase that lasted for all of two minutes—a very unfortunate two minutes for yours truly, as they happened to be the two minutes immediately following my birth.

"Look at her," Mom reportedly said, apparently reeling from the mind-altering effects of her pre-childbirth medications. "She's so colorful, so bright, so beautiful. She's like ... neon. That's it! We'll name her Neon. Neon Blue."

Why Dad, who was not under the influence of pre-childbirth medications or hallucinogens of any sort, didn't respond, "Sweetheart, isn't Neon Blue Greene a little much? Not to mention that neon can be so cheap, so garish, so in your face," is one of the unsolved mysteries of the world. My world, anyway.

Instead, he agreed with my blitzed-out mother and totally dumped Plan A.

Anna Rachel.

The name I was supposed to have.

Which goes a whole lot better with my younger brother's name, Jonathan. And the names of the temporarily insane parents, Rebecca and Michael.

It's no wonder that, deep-down, I feel as if random strangers found me in a crater on Mars and plunked me smack in the middle of this family. I sure as heck am nothing like the rest of them—except my Great-aunt Evelyn. Everyone says she's the old block to my chip because I inherited my being extra-annoyed by extra-annoying people directly from her. But as she and I will both tell you, it's for their own good.

For example, would Tyler Greevylane ever have stopped being so annoying if I'd rewarded him with my friendship in fifth grade for his nasal, whiny voice which he never, ever stopped using? Seriously. The kid never shut up.

While everyone else smiled at him and said "hi," then avoided him like a flock of passive aggressive sheep, I uninvited him to my birthday party after Mom made me invite him.

And I told him why.

True, this led to a little kerfuffle which ended with an insincere apology from me, but next thing I knew, he was off to the speech therapist for de-nasaling therapy. Then he grew six inches. And now he's practically cute. Which never would have happened if I'd been "nice" to him like everyone else.

I'd be positive I was adopted if not for my Great-aunt Evelyn. And the fact that I seem to have inherited my otherwise beautiful mother's weird, alien ears and pale, freckly skin. And my father's green eyes.

Forget I mentioned those—the ears, that is.

But, I mean, honestly.

Who names their kid after the color of a sports energy drink?

Wednesday After School, 3:05 p.m.
(2,390,100 seconds left to live)

"Neon," Maddie calls down the hall, her hands on her hips and her long black hair hitting her elbows. "Hurry! Amber's already late for softball, and I have an orthodontist appointment. We don't have much time to practice."

"What a mess." Genna, who is holding my books, leans down to fish my long-lost water bottle, a stack of stuck-together papers that I'm hoping is my missing math homework, and a bunch of Reese's Peanut Butter Cup wrappers from the heap on the floor in front of my bright-orange locker while I dig to the bottom for my white cheer shoes.

"Got 'em!" I shove everything back in, slam the door shut, then glance up and see Weird Bobby. He's standing in front of his bright-orange locker, two down from mine, staring inside. He hasn't moved since we got here, and he won't move until everyone leaves. That's how he acts in a crowd. He's just there in the background. Like elevator music.

"Do you need help finding something, Bobby?" Genna asks in her usual, kind way.

He doesn't answer.

I walk over and look inside his locker. It's empty, except for five books organized from tallest to smallest on the top shelf. "Your locker sure is a lot neater than mine."

He opens his eyes extra wide as he keeps staring. His eyebrows slide a touch closer, into an almost frown.

Genna's liquid-chocolate eyes and supercomputer brain take it all in.

Blink. Click. Information Noted.

Blink. Click. Information Stored.

"Neon! Genna! C'mon!" Maddie calls again.

"Well, see you tomorrow." I smile at Weird Bobby, but his eyebrows don't move another millimeter. Then Genna and I jog outside.

"Over here!" Amber stands on top of the second row of bleachers and waves. She's shorter than the rest of us and convinced she'll have a growth spurt any day now. I'm not so sure, considering that her parents aren't giving the Green Giant a run for his money.

I sit next to Amber and tie my left shoe. Maddie, who's sitting in front of us, leaps up as the boys' track team runs by. A tall boy, whose dark brown bangs bounce across his forehead, lopes in our direction.

"Ne-on, it's Jay-ake." Maddie waves at him, rolling her fingers one by one in a fan-like move.

I wave without looking as I tie my right shoe. No way am I giving Maddie a hint that sometimes—more like hardly ever—I think Jake's kind of cute, but mostly I'm not sure how I feel about

16

him at all anymore.

"Cut it out, Maddie." Amber punches her lightly on the arm. "You're going to get that boy's hopes up! He'll think Neon told you to wave at him."

"Neon luuuuuvvvvvvvvssss Jake. She's just too shy to admit it."

"I can think of lots of words to describe Neon, but shy wouldn't be number one on my list," Genna says.

I leap over the bleachers and race to the field. "Let's go," I call. "We only have a few minutes to work on our new routine before Amber and Maddie have to go."

Wednesday After School Cheerleading Practice
Slap slap clap Slap slap clap
Slap slap clap Slap slap clap

Arms out Arms out Arms out Arms out
Arms up Arms up Arms up Arms up
Back Handsprings
One, Two, Three, Four

Go-o-o-o-o-o-o-o-o Chargers!
Jump Jump Jump Jump
Clap Clap Clap Clap

My Bedroom, Wednesday Night, 10:00 p.m.
Dear Smush,

Good Deed #2. Unplanned.

Today I helped Angel when Casey crashed into me and spilled his entire bottle of freezing cold neon blue Gatorade at lunch. It went all over everywhere, especially Angel.

Today, I saw Angel for the first time.

It made me feel like saltwater taffy, like my insides were twisted and tugged until they snapped into a whole new shape.

I wonder—if I never really looked at Angel before, what else—who else—have I not really been looking at?

The thing is—I'm nervous that Ms. Petrie might want me to actually become friends with Angel.

I hope Angel has a friend. Because underneath all those tears, her hazel eyes overflowed with goodness. There wasn't a glimmer or fleck of meanness in them.

But just because I helped her, it doesn't mean I want her friend to be me.

Not that I'd ever tease or make fun of her like that creep-o bully Eddie Rasmussen does. For one thing, Mom, aka the world's most devoted high school special ed teacher, would go ballistic if I did. And besides, the Special Eddies can't help how they are.

But a good deed is one thing. Spending the last 27 days and nine hours I have left to live actually being friends with Angel is another.

No Offense.

CHAPTER THREE

Thursday Morning, 4:00 a.m.
(27 days — 2,343,600 seconds — left to live)

I bolt up in bed and turn on my lamp. I'd fidgeted and tossed and turned, and couldn't fall asleep because of everything. But I finally must have — fallen asleep, I mean — because I woke up this second with an idea for a good deed. A really good deed. I think I got it because of what happened with Angel.

I grab my diary from my nightstand and start writing so I don't forget before morning.

Dear Smush,

I'm going to sit with Weird Bobby at lunch. He's the only kid at school who always sits alone in the cafeteria.

The geeks stick together, and the smart kids stick together except the ones who overlap with the band kids. The cheerleaders sit with the girls' soccer team — except sometimes Genna sits with the Black History Club because she's president, and sometimes she sits with the theater kids because she stars in all the school plays.

And, of course, Angel and Casey and any other special ed kids who need help getting lunch sit together with Ms. Petrie.

But there isn't a Weird Miguel or a Weird Heather to sit with Weird Bobby. He's in a Weird Bobby clique all his own. So, just for today, I'm going to walk right over to his table and sit down.

I'll let you know how it goes.

Lunchtime, Thursday, 11:45 a.m.
(2,315,700 seconds left to live)

"Hi." I stand in front of Weird Bobby with my tray. His brown hair is a greasy mess. His used — as in, Goodwill, not vintage — Polo by Ralph Lauren has pizza stains on the collar. His zipped-up sweatshirt is discount-store gray, and his glasses are held together with duct tape and a paper clip on one side. Definitely not living in Angel's house, this guy.

I don't move. He rotates his pale blue eyes so hard to the side I'm afraid they'll get stuck inside his ears. Weird Bobby never makes eye contact, but if I wait long enough, he'll talk.

Eventually.

I think.

"Hail—" He stops so short, it's like he ripped out the emergency brake.

Silence.

I begin tapping the side of my tray with my thumb, patience not being my most stupendous virtue. I look at him and raise my eyebrows to show the question marks in my eyes. I can't get him to even glance my way.

"—Neon, Queen of the Cafeteria. What's going on?" he asks at last, his words tumbling out so fast they crash into each other at warp speed. But his voice reminds me of someone.

Me. It reminds me of me.

Right.

This is one reason Weird Bobby is so weird. He always knows what other kids will say before they say it. And he says it. Out loud. In their voices.

Maybe I'll skip Weird Bobby. I think this was a better idea at four a.m. alone in my room than live and in person. I could start over with a more realistic good deed. Like, world peace.

As I turn to leave, I hear, "Be my guest."

He motions to the empty metal folding chair opposite him at the ketchup-stained table in a very un-Weird-Bobby-like way.

My feet freeze. I never knew feet literally freeze when they don't want to do something.

"Not getting cold feet, are you?" he asks.

On the bright side, I'll bet sitting with Weird Bobby counts as a bunch of good deeds and gets me Triple Bonus Points for my Miracle. I pull out the chair and sit.

The entire cafeteria gets so quiet you could hear a Dorito crunch clear across the room.

Everyone is listening. And looking. And wondering if I'm

about to do something.

Something funny, or outrageous, or mean, but since outright mean isn't my style, Everyone is waiting.

"How about those chicken nuggets?" I punch the air as if we just won a gold medal in the Chicken Nugget Olympics.

Weird Bobby laser stares at the nuggets on his plate. "Here." He holds one out without looking at me.

His fingernails are dirty and jagged. I don't think his grown-ups at home ever make him wash or cut them. But he's wearing passable jeans. Not starched and ironed or especially clean like Angel's, but not total dork, either. His cool—as in, life is not fair *so* cool—older brother's hand-me-downs, I bet.

"No, thanks. I have lunch." I take a bite of my veggie burger on a whole wheat bun. It's the only food in the cafeteria that doesn't have moldy sponge smell. As opposed to the neon yellow mac and cheese which looks and smells worse than yesterday's vomit and is glued next to those rubber chicken nuggets on Weird Bobby's plate.

There are murmurs in the cafeteria now.

I still don't stand up, and the murmurs turn to rumbles. Maddie—who, surprisingly, if you ask me, is nicer to weird and annoying people than I am but doesn't go out of her way to be nice to everyone the way Genna does—stands and looks around. Her shiny black hair swings back and forth as she walks over to Jordan, Sarah, and Katie and sits at their table.

I wish my hair would be all shiny and swingy when I walk.

Anyway, Jordan is pretty, but she always has B.O. Sarah writes funny stories that our teachers read to the rest of us. She'd almost be popular if she didn't laugh like a horse. Katie's okay. She just has bad taste in friends, which makes her a member of the N.B.A.—Nerds by Association.

Maddie whispers to Jordan, who nods and scoots closer to her.

The entire cafeteria is mesmerized.

No one has the power that Maddie and I do. Except Genna, whose power is in a league of its own.

For example, one snowy, cold day last December, I wore my purple and orange Wilson-Pike Chargers flip-flops to school because I was late and couldn't find my new sneakers, my old sneakers, or my boots. The next day, all the clueless kids in my class, aka everyone except Genna, Maddie, and Amber, copied me and wore their purple and orange Wilson-Pike Chargers flip-flops to school. It's a wonder there wasn't an epidemic of frostbite.

"Uuuuse your powwwwwer for goooooood," a sarcastic voice that sounds suspiciously like Great-aunt Evelyn drawls in my head.

I ignore the voice and look at Weird Bobby.

"I'm going to die in twenty-seven days," I say.

Weird Bobby shifts his laser stare to the neon yellow gelatinous clumps of mac and cheese glooped together now into a solid brick on his plate. He squishes his lips into a tight, straight line.

"You're supposed to say something," I say.

He doesn't talk.

I finish my veggie burger.

He still doesn't talk.

I finish my orange juice.

He pulls a tiny, thick square of paper from his left front jeans pocket and unfolds it eight times. Like magic, it becomes a gimongous sheet of paper with a giant chart. Sentences, arrows, and dates crisscross in illegible scrawls all over.

He doesn't look at me as he slips a forest green fine point marker out from behind an actual pocket protector clipped to one of his sweatshirt pockets. He circles the marker in the air above the giant chart, zooms down to Lunchtime, First Talk, Seventh Grade, and draws a green asterisk.

"That's not what you were supposed to say." He points to a spot on the chart.

I lean across the table. According to Weird Bobby's chart, my next sentence was supposed to be, "How do you like Ms. Denning?"

It's true. That's one of the first things every seventh grader asks every other seventh grader because Everyone has her and Everyone either totally loves or absolutely hates her quirky sense of humor.

Looks like I threw Weird Bobby for a loop.

"That's not a funny joke." His eyes flit back to the imitation food on his plate.

"It's not a joke," I say. "It's a secret. No one knows."

He spears a lonely piece of crusted-over, dried up macaroni with his fork. But he doesn't put it in his mouth.

I watch Weird Bobby as he stares at his food.

And the strangest thought whispers deep inside my brain as if I've known it all along.

I can tell Weird Bobby anything.

Everything.

Even if Weird Bobby tells, no one will believe him.

So I do. I tell him all about what I heard. I tell him about my parents. I tell him about my good deed plan to get a Miracle.

He sits there, holding his breath and staring at that crusty, shriveled piece of macaroni as if the fate of humankind rested on his decision—to eat, or not to eat.

"Take a breath, okay?" I say. His face is so red from not breathing that I'm afraid he'll asphyxiate himself.

"You're saying all the wrong sentences. There is only ... a two point three seven six percent chance that you'd do that."

"Die?"

"No. Say the wrong sentence."

"How'd you come up with two point three seven six?" I ask.

He starts twisting the fingers on his left hand, the one not holding the fork, as if he's counting. One, two, three, four, five. One, two, three, four, five. Over and over again.

I scrape my chair backwards on the linoleum floor so I'm right in his line of vision. "Well?" I stare at him eyeball to eyeball, but it's like invisible curtains just snapped shut and his eyeballs aren't open for business.

"Okay. Fine." I pick up my tray.

How did this even happen? I was only supposed to sit with Weird Bobby. Not get sucked into his Weird Bobby Universe.

"See you around," I—very predictably—say. That should make his chart all happy again.

I walk across the cafeteria. As I pass their tables, my classmates buzz with excitement at this upheaval in the seventh grade social order. I toss my juice bottle into the recycling bin, dump my tray, and glance back at the table.

My veggie burger twists and flips in my stomach.

Weird Bobby is still there, staring at his hand suspended in mid-air and that single shriveled piece of macaroni teetering on his fork.

Mrs. Valentine, Thursday After School

I'm totally off balance for the rest of the day, like I'm dangling at some strange angle from the ceiling, looking upside down at my life. After being totally weirded out by my lunch with Weird Bobby, I need a dose of normal. I need Mrs. Valentine.

I rush home, relieved that this is a Thursday without after-school activities because there's no way I could face cheerleading practice. I dash up the three steps to the back porch, drop my backpack inside, and spot an aluminum foil-covered paper plate on the kitchen counter. I hold it to my nose, close my eyes, and inhale. Mom's banana bread. With a yellow Post-it attached that says For Mrs. Valentine. Thanks, Sweetie. xoxo

I grab the banana bread and go outside. The clouds are gone, and the sun is shining the perfect color of bright that happens only in May, just enough for the world to look new and crisp, but not so much that you have to squint to notice.

Rainbow bounces past me and we run to Mrs. Valentine's house. It's a Cape Cod style house with sky blue shutters. We rush through the gate and up the pebble path to her midnight blue front door. She opens it as soon as I knock.

"Hi, Mrs. Valentine."

"Neon, dear." She smiles. "How was school today?"

"Fine, thanks," I say out of habit, and walk into her living room.

Last year, Mrs. Valentine got sick and tired of her dark "old lady furniture." She went straight to Bullerdeen's Furniture Store and bought a bright red sectional couch, a Matisse print, and a new coffee table, which she said is a copy of something called mid-century modern. She said if she'd kept the genuine mid-century modern coffee table she bought at a thrift store when she and Mr. Valentine first got married, she'd be practically a millionaire.

Rainbow looks at her with Soppy Dog Loveface. "C'mon, girl." She gives her a pat, and Rainbow trots, tail up, right behind her into the kitchen. "Let's get your treat."

I put the aluminum foil-covered paper plate on the kitchen counter. "Mom asked me to bring this over."

Mrs. Valentine peeks under a corner of the foil, and sighs. "She's a gem, that mother of yours. You know, she makes her banana bread with applesauce, no sugar, just for me."

Every Halloween, Mrs. Valentine gives out full-sized candy bars, not the twerpy, fun-sized ones. And every Halloween, she says, "Take a few more, kiddo. Can't have leftovers. I have to watch my sugar, you know."

This from the woman whose living room always smells of the chocolate chip cookies she makes for the Dweeb and me. That's its number one smell. Number two is frying onions and garlic when she's making spaghetti sauce. And when she's not cooking at all, which is pretty much never, I smell black licorice when I breathe in, but when I breathe out again, I smell tangerine.

"Neon, dear, are you feeling okay?"

Mrs. Valentine walks back into the living room, sits, and pats the couch for me to join her. Rainbow plops on the floor next to us on the small blue and gray braided rug that's just for her.

The red velvet, heart-shaped Russell Stover chocolates box that Mr. Valentine gave to Mrs. Valentine on their first Valentine's

Day is on the coffee table in front of us. It's still decorated with the red, silver, and pink origami heart-shaped notes that Mr. Valentine made. He placed a note on top of each chocolate inside, too.

The red hearts make a promise. Like *"I promise we'll go to the movies on Saturday night."* The silver hearts say mushy stuff like *"Girl of my Dreams, Love of my Life."*

But the pink hearts are the best of all. They're for making a secret wish. Mrs. Valentine used to close her eyes and hold a pink heart close to her own heart for as many seconds as she thought it took. She taught the Dweeb and me to do it the same way.

The chocolates are always new, of course. And when we were little, Mrs. Valentine added some brand new promises just for us.

I want to make a secret wish, but I'm worried that Mrs. Valentine will know for sure that something's wrong since she's already asked. Instead, I choose a red heart and hand it to her.

"The promise you've won is," she opens the heart and reads, "A dozen chocolate chip cookies!"

I glance at the clock on her fireplace mantle, hoping she won't notice. "I'd better save the cookies for another day," I say, then can't believe I said it. I've never not wanted Mrs. Valentine's chocolate chip cookies right away before. Ever.

"It's getting late. I'll bet you're feeling a little anxious about your homework," Mrs. Valentine says.

I nod. I'm feeling anxious, all right. Just not about my homework.

"C'mon, Rainbow." I stand and pet her. "Time to go home."

Mrs. Valentine stands, too, to walk us to the door. "Stop by tomorrow. I'll warm you up a slice of your mom's banana bread to go with the cookies."

"I'm not sure if I can. I have practice and ..."

Rainbow tilts her head. One ear flops down as she gives me her Get-with-the-Program-Neon Dog Stare. She turns, and I follow her gaze around Mrs. Valentine's house, from the Hershey's Kisses in the small crystal bowl and the collection of ceramic animal salt and pepper shakers displayed on a shelf in the kitchen, to the perfectly placed photographs of smiling people on the refrigerator, including the Dweeb's and my school pictures from every year since preschool.

And I wonder.

I never met Mr. Valentine. I guess he died a long time ago. It's such a happy-looking house, but it can't have been all sky blue shutters and pale pink roses for Mrs. Valentine.

I never thought before about whether she needed a visit. I always just thought about if I wanted one.

Or a chocolate chip cookie.

"Sure. I'll come by after cheerleading tomorrow if it's not too late, or on Saturday morning when I'm home from my sleepover. Thanks, Mrs. Valentine." I look at Rainbow.

She blinks her eyes. And her mouth curves into a great big Rainbow smile.

Rainbow, Best Dog Ever

Rainbow is one part Labrador Retriever and a bunch of parts mystery dog. Officially, she belongs to our whole family. But everyone knows she's mine.

She came to live with us — most especially me — when we were both twelve weeks old. Mom says when we met, Rainbow thought I was a puppy, and I thought she was a baby. She was so gentle that Mom and Dad let her cuddle with me in my crib, which, looking back on it, doesn't strike me as award-winning parental judgment. But she didn't suffocate me, and I didn't squish her, so it worked out okay.

Rainbow used to lick orange baby food squash off my fingers right down to the last disgusting lump because she knew I hated it. I used to eat giant clumps of crunchy kibble beef bits from her bowl because we both liked it — until the day we got caught with dried up orange squash streaked across her wet black nose and crunchy kibble drool dripping down my one-year-old chin.

For my entire life, she's rescued me from that yucky squash, and smelly Brussels sprouts, and slimy asparagus. Not to mention loneliness, which never sticks around for long because Rainbow makes it melt away.

She's the best rescue dog ever, like Lassie, Snoopy, and Scooby-Doo all rolled into one.

Only better.

My Bedroom, Thursday Night, 10:30 p.m.

Dear Smush,

Sitting with Weird Bobby was supposed to be a good deed if ever there was one. As in, a drums beating, horns blasting, Nobel prize winning, monster good deed.

Instead, I can't get the picture of his miserable, frozen face and that shriveled-up piece of macaroni on his fork out of my mind.

I shouldn't have told him the whole plan. I'm kind of worried he figured out that he was a good deed, and it hurt his feelings—which would pretty much ruin the point of the Weird Bobby good deed plan.

When a good deed goes bad, is it the thought that counts?

Or is it worse than if I never tried at all?

At least I can always count on Mrs. Valentine to make me feel better. But I don't think even Mrs. Valentine's pink hearts and secret wishes have enough power in Good Deed Land to get me my Miracle.

Especially if my own good deeds keep going bad.

CHAPTER FOUR

Pre-Algebra, Friday Afternoon, 2:00 p.m.
(26 days — 2,221,200 seconds — left to live)

"Katie, number six. Tommy, number seven," Ms. Tucker calls them to the whiteboard.

Amber's next, but she's staring at her homework as if it's in pig Latin hieroglyphics. Math's never been her thing, but she hit a concrete wall this year with pre-algebra. Genna, on the other hand, whizzed through algebra last semester, so now she's in an advanced geometry class set up for her and two genius eighth graders.

As Tommy starts writing on the board, his sleeve slips down to his elbow. His arm is a mess of red blotches and blisters.

I nudge Maddie. "When did all that pop out? I didn't see it in homeroom. Did you?"

"Beats me. I try not to look at him in homeroom," she says.

"Ooooh, Tommy." Katie scoots a couple of feet away from him. "Move over."

"Katie!" Ms. Tucker scolds.

Katie crinkles her face. "It's gross."

Ms. Tucker walks over, pushes up the navy blue glasses perched halfway down her nose, and examines Tommy's arm. "Poison ivy?"

He nods.

"That's a bad-looking rash. Have you seen the doctor?" she asks.

The rash. I forgot about the rash.

It began four or five weeks ago on my arms. Then it moved to my neck and belly. I thought it was poison ivy from the woods behind Amber's backyard, but when oatmeal baths and calamine lotion didn't make it feel better, Mom took me to the dermatologist.

Dr. Fortensa said it didn't look like poison ivy, poison oak, or poison anything. She said when they don't know, it's called a non-specific rash, and she gave me a prescription for a cream that worked so fast I forgot all about it.

Mom had an appointment with the dermatologist, too, that day. At least, she told me she did when she went into the examining room as soon as I was done.

But what if Mom's was a fake appointment? What if she and Dr. Fortensa were really talking about a secret incurable kid disease that starts with a rash?

Because if it wasn't poison something, what was it?

Juvenile Rashilitis: A non-specific itchy rash that begins on the arms but can later appear anywhere on the body. While it generally resolves on its own, in rare cases, Juvenile Rashilitis is the first symptom of the incurable Juvenile Fatalitis which is known to afflict only twelve-year-old girls.

Specifically, twelve-year-old girls named Neon, who, from the outside, live picture-perfect lives in quaint New England towns, but actually—

"Neon ... Neon!" Ms. Tucker pats my shoulder. She looks as if she's been there for a while. "Are you with us? You're up. Number nine."

Friday After School Cheerleading Practice
Slap slap clap Slap slap clap
Slap slap clap Slap slap clap

Front Flip Back Flip Front Flip Back Flip
Front   Back
            Flip
Front   Back
Flip   Flip
Back Flip Front Flip Back Flip Front Flip

Go-o-o-o-o-o-o-o-o Chargers!
Jump Jump Jump Jump
Clap Clap Clap Clap

Friday Evening Sleepover At Maddie's House After School And Cheerleading Practice

"Pepperoni and mushroom, or just mushroom?" Genna asks again, plunking down next to Amber on Maddie's futon. We're all wearing the same purple and orange flannel p.j. pants—our school colors—for our every-Friday-night-after-cheerleading-practice sleepover.

"No, peppers," says Maddie. "No, wait. Pepperoni, onions, and peppers. But skip the pepperoni on one."

"I want a slice of extra cheese and—" I bounce so hard the aquamarine comforter slides off the bed.

"Wait," says Maddie. "Make mine—"

"I give up." Genna hands me her pen and paper. "You do it."

I pass the pen and paper back to Genna. "Here. Write what you want on the list."

She narrows her eyes at me. "Why didn't I think of that?"

"Okay," I say when everyone is done writing. "Tell me if this is right."

Pizza List
1 anchovy and olive
1 cheese
1 pepperoni, onion, and pepper
1 onion and pepper
1 mushroom and sausage
1 extra cheese
1 mushroom, onion, and green pepper

"Anchovy and olive?" Maddie flicks the purple and orange rubber bands on her braces. "Seriously?"

Genna shrugs. "I'm craving anchovies."

"And olives?" Amber makes a face as she texts our order to Pizza Palazzo.

"Scrabble or Ouija Board?" Maddie holds up one, then the other.

"Scrabble," I shout, too fast and too loud. I glance at Genna and catch her studying me.

I hate Scrabble. Everyone knows I hate Scrabble. I can never think of a five-letter word to save my life.

To. Save. My. Life.

A rush of sadness whooshes through my body then lands with a thud inside my chest. I close my eyes and concentrate to chase that sadness away.

"What? No TikTok?" Amber puts down her phone and widens her bluish-green eyes. "Did the Earth start spinning in reverse or something?"

"Funny," I say, considering that Amber is the most phone-addicted of all of us. "I'm trying to be flexible. I know you guys would rather play Scrabble now and do the Ouija board later, when it's dark and spoooooky. Think of it as your early birthday present, Amber."

Still, I'm going to have to make this the longest Scrabble game ever because Maddie's Ouija Board is seriously psychic. There's no way it would keep my secret when I can't even push it away right now.

"Neon?" Maddie waves her hand in front of my face. "Did you hear me?"

"Huh?" I say.

"Would you go to the Snowflake Dance with Jake Carlisle if he asks you? I know he wants to because he asked Mike to ask me if I thought you'd say yes."

"Not sure." I try to keep a blank expression on my face. "I'm kind of busy. So, Amber," I say, "what are you doing for your birthday? Besides our sleepover next week, I mean."

When Amber hesitates and looks down for a second, Genna jumps in. "No changing the subject. Since when are you too busy for the Snowflake Dance? We've been waiting to go since fifth grade!"

Maddie raises her left eyebrow. "Since when are you too busy for Jake?"

"How could anyone be too busy for Jake?" Amber asks.

"I dunno. He got all long and gangly this year. I should have gone out with him last year when he was more ... cuddly."

Amber snorts, and chocolate milk rockets out of her nose. "Cuddly? That's how you would have described Jake last year?"

"He really is the cutest boy in seventh grade," says Genna.

"And he luuuuuvs you," says Amber.

"And he's sex-eeee." Maddie swivels her hips. "Ooooh, you know what you should do?" She hugs her stuffed giraffe to her lips. *Smooch, Smooch, Smack.* "You should invite him to your cabin at the lake!" *Smooch, Smoo—*

"Gross!" I throw a lime green pillow at her, mid-kiss.

"Maddie!" Genna and Amber say at the same time, but Genna's lip is quivering as she tries not to laugh.

Maddie's the only one of us who's ever kissed a boy. She told us that she and Mike kissed three times at Mike's big brother's birthday party in December. Since that was five months ago, I bet they've kissed dozens of times by now.

"It's true," Genna says. "Jake can't keep his eyes off you. Every time you pass him in the hall with that aloof look of yours and the same 'Hi' you give everyone else, his head droops like a lovesick giraffe's."

Maddie flops the giraffe's head up and down, up and down.

"Aloof? I'm not aloof," I say.

Amber snorts again, sending more chocolate milk out of her nose. This is one of the reasons she is only my third best friend.

The doorbell rings. Maddie and Amber rush to get it.

"Neez?" Genna scans my face. "Is everything okay?"

A pain shoots down my arms. I fight the urge to go statue still. "Sure." I nod.

"It's just ... for the past few days you've been acting a little bit ... different." Genna, being Genna, is treading carefully so she doesn't hurt my feelings.

"I'm nervous about eighth grade. You know, the way everyone keeps talking about it."

"See? Even that's different. You're never nervous about anything. And we'll be the oldest kids in school. It's going to be awesome."

My cheeks burn like they're being barbequed from the inside out, but there's no way to stop. I've never learned how to unblush once I start blushing.

"It's hormones! I know it is. It figures you'd be the first to have heavy-duty teenage hormones before the rest of us," says Genna.

The aroma of pizza drifts into Maddie's room with Amber trailing behind, carrying the box. "Pizza delivery," she announces. "Seven slices, one Dr. Pepper, one orange juice, and two glasses of water."

Amber hands a red and white plastic tablecloth to Genna. I help her spread it out on the rug, then pass around the plates and close my eyes as I take a hot, cheesy bite of my mushroom, onion, and green pepper slice.

We chew quietly for a couple of minutes before Amber asks, "What's everybody taking next year? Latin, Mandarin, Spanish, or French?"

Maddie sighs. "I'll probably stick with Spanish. I've had it for two years, and at least I'm still passing."

"I'm taking French and Mandarin," says Genna. "It would be so cool to live in Paris during college."

"College!" says Amber. "How can you think about college? We haven't even finished middle school."

"How about you, Neez?" asks Genna. "Sticking with Latin, or joining the modern world?"

"Huh?"

"Your language?" Genna waves her hand in front of my face. "Next year?"

Next year.

My stomach pounds. The room begins to spin.

Or maybe I'm spinning. I can't tell.

"I think I'm going to be sick." I rush to the bathroom.

"Careful!"

"Slow down!"

Maddie and Genna are somehow right next to me, catching me as I crumple onto the black and white tile floor. The room is

34

spinning so fast now I can't get up, but the urge to puke has passed.

"I'm calling your mom." Maddie whips out her phone.

Genna holds my arm and helps me stand. "You look awfully pale."

"It must be food poisoning!" Amber rushes to take my other arm as they help me walk back to Maddie's room.

Genna looks at my paper plate. "Not likely. She only had one bite. Probably the stomach flu."

I kneel down, squeezing my arms across my stomach, then bend flat from my waist until my forehead touches the soft turquoise rug.

The dizziness starts to go away, and I feel a little better. I sit and watch Genna pretend to concentrate as she sets up Scrabble for three instead of four, but I know her genius mathematical mind is clicking away. The problem is, I'm becoming a puzzle, and no one in the seventh grade is better than Genna at solving puzzles.

I could tell her.

She wouldn't tell.

Not only is Genna smart, beautiful, and kind, but she always keeps secrets.

Always.

I clutch my stomach tighter.

I haven't even thought about how Genna is going to feel when I die.

But I'm not ready.

I'm not ready to see her face when I tell her.

I'm not ready to say, "Have a nice life without me."

My phone vibrates. "My mom's here."

Genna hands me my backpack and takes my arm to hold me steady.

"I'm sorry," I say as we go downstairs.

Genna scans my face, and I see her eyes sending information straight to her brain. "Don't be sorry. It's not your fault you're sick."

Sick. I don't even know what that word means anymore.

"We'll do the Ouija Board another time," she says.

"Another time." I nod, as pinpoint shivers begin prickling down my arms.

"You're getting goosebumps. You'd better go." She opens the front door. "You might have a fever."

I turn to look at Genna and make myself smile, but as I do, I gasp with pain. Genna grabs my arm again as my stomach spasms with the hardest kick yet.

And as my stomach pounds, I know.

I can't count on there being another time—for anything—anymore.

The Snowflake Dance

It happened last year at the seventh grade Snowflake Dance. Raymond Whiting and Tiffany Ramone were caught butt—and every other body part—naked in a stall in the girls' bathroom, just about to go all the way.

I was not happy to know this last year when I was eleven and only sort of got where the heck they were going all the way to.

Now that I've had Life Skills and get exactly where they might have been going, I'm even less happy to know it. But I'm mystified by how they both fit in that bathroom stall without crushing each other to death. And it wasn't even the extra wide handicapped one.

Ms. Goodworthy, our principal, took full responsibility for the whole mess.

She apologized for the lyrics in the pop, hip hop, and rock 'n' roll songs the DJ played at the dance, which to this day she believes were the reason Raymond and Tiffany were doing whatever they were doing in that bathroom stall.

Honestly. It's hardly Ms. Goodworthy's fault that Raymond and Tiffany's hanky-panky was in a pre-teen league of its own.

But thanks to them and their butt-nakedness, Ms. Goodworthy

decreed that dances are a thing of the past at Wilson-Pike Middle School.

This did not go over well with this year's Seventh Grade Student Council. We voted to have the Snowflake Dance in February anyway.

Ms. Goodworthy vetoed us.

Unlike the United States Congress, we didn't get to override her veto, so we asked the Student Council Advisor, Ms. Blakely, to talk to the President of the PTA, who happens to be Maddie's mom.

Maddie's mom talked to Ms. Goodworthy.

Ms. Goodworthy held her ground.

We held our ground right back at her.

By the next morning, there was rebellion in the air.

First, all the seventh graders were mysteriously too busy to participate in the annual wrapping paper sale.

Ms. Goodworthy didn't give an inch.

Then one homeroom sat-in and refused to leave for a whole hour—a dramatic statement even if that hour happened to be during the previously mentioned and universally despised Life Skills class.

Still Ms. Goodworthy didn't budge.

That's when a few of us skated right up to the cliff of the dark side. There were rumblings of a plan to blow the Achievement Exams on purpose, and some tattletale suggested that those rumblings started with the Student Council Officers, aka Genna, Amber, and me.

Well, everyone knows Genna is entirely too well-behaved to suggest anything that awful. So that left Amber and me, about to go to prison for life when all we wanted was to have the Snowflake Dance. But since no one could pin that rap on us for sure, we slid out of that scrape without doing time.

But I think that's what did it. I guess Ms. Goodworthy, who even I could see was trying to do the right thing even if I didn't agree with her, got the message that maybe she had gone too far.

She proposed that we have one dance, an Oldies Spring Fling, during the last week of school. She gave us a list of permissible oldies. It was a very short list.

Bach's Minuet in G

We said it had to be the Snowflake Dance on a Saturday night in February, with music from the current millennium.

After weeks of heated negotiations, we finally came to terms:

1. The seventh grade will have the Snowflake Dance on a weekday night in May at the end of the year.

2. Students may slow dance together to Ms. Goodworthy-approved songs which will include some rock 'n' roll oldies.

3. There will be no kissing.

Okay with me. Though I'm beginning to wonder about this kissing thing. A little.

4. There will be no grinding.

As if that's happening with our class. Yuck.

5. There will be separate bathroom breaks for girls and boys, and chaperones stationed at every bathroom door.

And that's how we're having the Snowflake Dance the Wednesday after next, after all.

Cozy Night, Friday Night After The Sleepover

"Hey J.B.," I say, walking into the family room a few minutes later. "What's up?"

His eyes are glued to his video game on the TV as his fingers zip across the controller. Rainbow's eyes are glued to the TV, too. "Mrs. Valentine came over for dinner."

"She did?" I say, my heart sinking.

"She didn't stay long," he says with a shrug, "but she brought cookies."

I can't believe I missed Mrs. Valentine because of my sleepover, and missed the rest of my sleepover because I felt sick.

As I watch the Dweeb play for a while, and watch Rainbow watching him, a thought teases around the edges of my brain, and all the worry of the past three days begins melting away. I must have misheard what my parents were saying Wednesday morning. I'm sure I did. They couldn't—they wouldn't—hide something so big from me. Not when everything is so normal.

"How come you're not at your sleepover?" the Dweeb asks without looking my way.

All three of us lean sideways as he flips the red car and it zooms upside down across the screen to the finish line.

"I wasn't feeling great at Maddie's house. Besides," I punch his arm, "I missed you."

"Are you sick?"

"Nope. Not anymore. Wanna have Cozy Night?"

He puts down the controller and looks at me. "Tonight?"

I nod. "Now that I'm feeling okay, Mom and Dad decided to go out for a little while."

His face lights up. I'll bet making my little brother happy doesn't count as a good deed if it's this easy—if I even need to do good deeds anymore.

Plus, I love Cozy Night.

Sometimes it's just the Dweeb and me, sometimes we invite friends, and sometimes our whole family gets into p.j.s early on a Saturday night. We always watch movies and get to order Chinese food unless Mom makes her famous vegetarian lasagna. Even the Dweeb, who's never met a vegetable he doesn't hate, scarfs it down.

"I'll make the popcorn. You find Mom's chocolate."

The secret stash of the very same Mom who would feed us a steady diet of alfalfa sprouts and broccoli if Dad didn't sneak junk food and Mrs. Valentine didn't slip cookies past enemy lines now and then.

"Find it fast, J.B. Mom and Dad won't be out long."

"No way, Neon. Last time, the Cadbury bars were hidden inside Mom's pantyhose. And," he wrinkles his nose, "the Kit Kats were under her bras."

"Good point." I nod. "You make the popcorn and melt the

butter. I'll search Mom's hiding places. But don't set the kitchen on fire again."

"I never set it on fire," he calls after me as I run upstairs.

Technically, he's right. The Dweeb set the pan on fire last time he made popcorn, which would have set the whole house on fire—not to mention the popped kernels rocketing all over the place—if I hadn't slapped a cover on top of those flames in the nick of time.

I used to think popcorn was the grossest thing ever. Then, one day last year, Mom forbade Dad from buying the packaged stuff and made the old-fashioned kind in a pot with oil. It was love at first bite. Turns out it's just fake-butter microwave popcorn that leaves me half a breath short of puking every time I smell it.

I dig through Mom's pajamas until I find them: a bag of mini-Reese's hidden inside the sleeve of her red flannel nightshirt at the bottom of the drawer. I feel the top of something rectangular underneath the bag. Hoping for a Cadbury bar, I reach further inside to get it.

When a Loved One Is Dying
Talking to your Child about Death
Grief and Grieving
Three brochures.

I stare as tears sting my eyes, but I don't ... I can't ... read them. It's as if I've just found out all over again.

"Neon," the Dweeb yells, "the popcorn's ready."

The room spins around me. I sit on Mom and Dad's bed, flop my head down over my knees, and breathe to stop the nauseousness I felt at Maddie's house from starting all over again.

"Ne-on!"

Nothing's changed. It was only a few minutes. A few minutes of thinking everything's okay. Of thinking I'm okay.

"Be right there," I say.

I breathe in and out, again and again, until the room stops spinning and my heart isn't pounding quite so hard. I hurry to Mom's drawer, stuff the brochures back into the sleeve of her red flannel nightshirt, and check my face for tear stains in the mirror above her dresser.

"Ow!" The Dweeb pulls his hand away from the hot handle as I walk into the kitchen. "What took you so long?" He grabs a potholder and pours the popcorn into a bowl.

"Good job, Dweeb-o. You didn't even burn the place down. Hold these for a second." My voice is shaky as I hand him the mini-Reese's, but the Dweeb doesn't seem to notice. Then I sprinkle salt and drizzle the melted butter over the popcorn.

"What'll it be? *Mr. Deeds, Harry Potter, Mike Mulligan,* or *Minions*?" I ask.

We always start with *Mr. Deeds, Harry Potter,* or some other old movie from Mom and Dad's DVD collection. It's a tradition— except when Mom and Dad are home because *Mr. Deeds* is PG-13, and they think the Dweeb's too young to watch it.

"Mr. Deeds."

We get comfy under the afghan on the La-Z-Boy loveseat in the family room. Rainbow plops down on the rug in front of us. I jump up to turn out the lights, and, grateful for the darkness, I start the movie.

The Dweeb laughs as soon as Adam Sandler is on the screen. He laughs at everything, even the sad parts, with his deep, gravelly, belly laugh, which makes him sound three years old and ninety years old at the same time. His laugh always cracks me up. Every time he laughs, I feel better.

Until I listened outside my parents' bedroom door on Wednesday morning, until I learned that the real secret of my life is that I barely have one—a life, that is—my only secret was that having Cozy Night with the Dweeb is my favorite thing in the world.

Go figure. I mean, the kid drives me nuts—literally. He eats peanut M&M's with his mouth open and cracks his knuckles at the same time to drive me crazy.

But he gets my jokes—all of them—and I get his—every single one of his dumb fart and burp seven-year-old-boy jokes. When he was little, he was the cuddliest giggle machine, and I was his favorite person in the universe.

I think I still kind of am.

I lick the butter and salt off my fingers and throw a kernel into Rainbow's mouth.

"Rainbow, catch!" I say, as she gulps it down.

Rainbow gets her own bowl of plain, unsalted, unbuttered popcorn because it's better for her. I'm pretty sure it's better for us that way, too, but now that I finally love popcorn, I'm sticking with the good stuff.

Rainbow looks up and barks. Then she races to the window and back, stopping short in front of me. She barks and barks, standing and staring at me.

"J.B., pause *Deeds* for a minute, okay?"

I walk to the window. The Dweeb grabs the afghan, wraps it around his shoulders, and hides behind me holding my waist. "Is it a zombie?" He pokes his head around to peek outside.

"How many times have I told you? There are no zombies in New England. They can't survive the winter. They freeze into sheets of ice, topple flat on the ground, and smash into a gazillion teeny, tiny zombie bits. It's probably Little Rufus."

Little Rufus is our neighbor's Giant Schnauzer who scares the heck out of everyone in the neighborhood, especially Rainbow.

I switch on the backyard floodlight and look outside. No sign of Little Rufus. No raccoons going through the trash. Not even a wayward moose following a muffin all the way from Alaska.

"Nothing out there, Rainbow." I scratch between her ears. "Coast is clear."

Rainbow looks at me with Worry Face.

She knows something's wrong. I don't know how she knows. But she always does.

I can't let the Dweeb see. Nothing's more of a giveaway when something's going on around this joint than Rainbow's Worry Face.

I scoop some extra-buttery popcorn into my hand, sit back

down on the loveseat, and hold out my palm. "Rainbow!"

She jumps between the Dweeb and me to gobble it up. Then she curls herself into a crescent moon, rests her head on my lap, and purrs.

Rainbow the purring dog, the Dweeb, and I huddle together under the afghan as we restart the movie.

"Dweeb-o?" I say a moment later.

He flops against my shoulder, so I shift him over to lie on the pillow. The Dweeb never makes it to the end. He always falls asleep at my favorite part—when Mr. Deeds saves the day by exposing the greedy bad guys who want to break up the company, sell off the pieces, and fire all the employees.

I don't notice when I fall asleep, except it must have been right at the beginning of *Harry Potter and the Sorcerer's Stone* because the last thing I remember is Dumbledore putting out the first streetlight with the Deluminator. When I wake up in the morning, the TV and lights are off, the afghan is crumpled on the floor, and the Dweeb is gone.

My teeth feel all fuzzy from not brushing last night, but I know Mom and Dad checked on us. They always do—to make sure we don't have any popcorn in our mouths so we don't choke and die.

Die.

Last night, once we finally settled down with *Mr. Deeds,* I forgot.

I completely, totally forgot.

My stomach throbs with pain, like someone slammed me with a dodgeball—or Casey's cafeteria tray—while I was sleeping.

"Mom?" I call. "Where is everybody?"

Silence.

I hold my stomach to push away the pain, but panic wraps itself around every nerve ending in my body. If I don't chase that panic away before it freezes my brain, I'll never think of enough good deeds to get my Miracle.

I close my eyes and take a deep breath. I try to think of something else—anything else—but no luck.

I open my eyes and see a note from Mom on the coffee table saying she went out early to buy a super-duper plumber's snake to fix the clogged sink in our laundry room, and the Dweeb has baseball practice today, which means Dad's there, too, since he's one of the coaches. His electrical company's slogan, Light Up Your Life—Call Team Greene, is on the back of the kids' T-shirts, just like it was for me when I played Little League.

There's nothing to do, but I'm not in the mood to call Genna, Maddie, or Amber. Besides, they all think I had the flu or something last night, and Genna will be suspicious if I'm better so soon.

At least Rainbow's still snuggled next to me. She's sleeping late, too. I turn her morning-dog-breath face away from mine and hold her tight.

Then I remember. I told Mrs. Valentine that I'd visit this weekend.

I unwrap my arms from around Rainbow's chest so I don't wake her and vault up the stairs two at a time to my room. I throw on a T-shirt, shorts, and flip-flops, brush my teeth, and hurry outside into the chilly May morning air. The kitchen door bangs shut as a blanket of black fur brushes against me and warms away the goosebumps on my legs.

"Rainbow! I thought you were asleep."

She pads alongside as we walk through the rose-covered gate to Mrs. Valentine's front door.

I ring the bell and wait. I ring it again. No answer.

I thought for sure she'd be home. I look down at Rainbow.

"I guess it's just you and me. Let's find those cookies Mrs. Valentine brought over last night and have some breakfast."

I bring Rainbow's bowl of kibble and my bowl of Oatie-Oats into the family room then go back to the kitchen to search for Mrs. Valentine's cookies. As I search the dish cabinet, I see a corner of a plastic bag peeking out from behind the pottery plates that we

44

use for special occasions. Jackpot! Three huge chocolate walnut cookies.

I sit down on the loveseat and take a bite of cookie. "Sorry, Rainbow. Chocolate isn't good for you."

She looks at me with the same exact expression Mom would give me if she were here. I'm pretty sure it translates to "And since when is chocolate good for *you*?"

I roll my eyes at Rainbow, but put down the cookie and have a spoonful of Oatie-Oats. I click on the TV, ready to start flipping channels, when a banner scrolls across the bottom of the screen.

Up Next: Surviving Cancer and Other Life-Threatening Diseases

My thumb hovers above the button on the remote control.

A little boy and his father appear on the screen, standing in front of a washing machine.

I wonder if the boy is sick.

Nope. The dad flashes a sparkly white smile and holds a bottle of detergent.

I daydream through the other commercials then realize that the show is on. Dr. Somebody is already talking.

"... essential. Absolutely. Patients' attitudes are a crucial element in their treatment. In fact," Dr. Somebody says as she looks directly into the camera, "this study shows that an optimistic, positive attitude can be a determining factor in whether a patient fully recovers."

I click off the TV.

That's the meanest, cruelest, most heartless thing I've ever heard.

A Joke, by Neon Blue Greene (Warning: I'm Not Too Good at Jokes)

Patient goes into doctor's office.

Doctor: "The bad news is you have a deadly disease and only, oh, let's say, twenty-eight days left to live. The good news is if you keep a positive attitude, you just might be cured!"

Patient, her shoulders heaving: "My family!" Sob. "My friends!"
Breathless gasp. "My stuffed porcupine collection!"

Okay, maybe the patient wouldn't say that. But I've had those porcupines since I was three.

Doctor: "Now, now. None of that! Remember, attitude. Attitude! It's all up to you!"

"You ... you ... you ..." will echo in the patient's nightmares every night for the next—the last—twenty-eight nights.

Talk about unfair. It makes me want to hurl.

Like I said. I'm not too good at jokes.

Monday Morning Before School

Dear Smush,

The human mind is truly strange. Or it could be just my mind that's strange.

I heard what Mom and Dad were whispering when Rainbow and I walked past their door. I saw the pamphlets Mom hid in her nightshirt. Even so, half the time, I forget the reason I'm doing good deeds in the first place and begin to wonder if I imagined the whole thing. Or if my parents were talking about where we're going on vacation. Or something.

But then I remember the nightmare I've had for three nights in a row.

Make that four. I had it again last night.

The Nightmare

I'm walking down our upstairs hallway when I get stuck outside my parents' bedroom. I begin to sink, a millimeter at a time, into the thick, goopy mud. With every millimeter I sink, my mom says, "I never thought we'd lose her so soon. I never thought we'd lose her so soon. I never thought we'd lose her so soon."

She says it over and over until she's said it 1000 times, and I've sunk 1000 millimeters. Just when I'm about to be swallowed into a whirling vortex, I wake up.

Except, I don't actually wake up. I dream that I'm awake and starting to sink all over again. I push and claw and dig my fists into the muddy walls, but the mud slurps me down like a humongous suction cup.

Then my alarm beeps, and I wake up. For real.

I guess my parents weren't talking about where we're going on vacation.

CHAPTER FIVE

Weird Bobby, Take Two, Lunchtime, Monday, 12:00 p.m.
(23 days—1,969,200 seconds—left to live)

I've been sitting across from Weird Bobby for at least five minutes. He hasn't looked up once or given any other sign that he knows I exist.

"I said, I'm scared."

Weird Bobby doesn't blink. He just keeps pulverizing the same chicken nugget he's had in his mouth the whole time.

"You're supposed to say something when someone tells you they're scared."

He shakes the ketchup bottle until it erupts like Vesuvius, burying the chicken nuggets on his plate under a slimy red blanket of imitation Heinz.

"You should tell Genna. Genna is your best friend." His words tumble out fast as a runaway train.

I play with the untouched veggie burger on my plate. Then I glance across the cafeteria at Genna sitting at our table with Maddie and Amber.

I know she's confused. Being especially nice to the weird kids isn't exactly what I'm famous for. It's like she's watching a personality transplant right before her eyes.

"You're scared," Weird Bobby continues quietly, "because ... you're going to die."

"Bingo. Ten points to the kid stating the obvious."

"But why?" Weird Bobby begins, ignoring my remark. "Why are you scared to die?"

"Why?" My voice rises. This kid has the emotional depth of a radiator.

I catch a glimpse of the sixth-grade dorks trying to eavesdrop from the table next to ours, their wide-eyed stares burning into my back.

"Death is a natural part of life." Weird Bobby keeps chewing, but he still doesn't look up. That chicken nugget must be completely liquefied by now.

"Thanks for the cliché," I say.

"Live for today. Enjoy life," says the killjoy boy who wouldn't know how to enjoy life if a truckload of cotton candy fell straight from the clouds into his mouth.

"You're a little late with that advice. Anyway, I don't agree. Life is a natural part of life. Then you die and go to heaven."

I hope. Because if there's no Miracle behind Door Number One, I'm counting on—

"There is no heaven," Weird Bobby interrupts my thought.

"There has to be," I say. "Heaven or maybe something else. Something like heaven."

"No. Heaven is not scientifically possible."

My cheeks grow hot. "That's a horrible thing to say to a dying person."

"It's no big deal. You're born. You live. You die. The circle of life."

"I hate you." I stand so fast my chair falls down behind me, but I don't stop to fix it. "This isn't the stupid *Lion King*. This is real life," I shout, my voice drowned out in the loud cafeteria. "My life."

I want to leave, to escape Weird Bobby. But as I reach for my missing napkin then wipe my wrist across my running nose, I can't help glancing at him. He doesn't look away from his ketchup-smothered mound of chicken nuggets, but he doesn't look angry, either. He just looks blank. Like the nothing he is.

"Stop staring!" The terrified sixth-grade dorks burn their popped-out eyeballs at the floor at my command.

I rush my tray to the conveyor belt. There's a lump in my throat, and it's not dried up veggie burger. It's the kind of lump that's about to make me cry in front of everyone.

No way will I let a Nobody Nothing like Weird Bobby make me break my never-cry-in-front-of-anyone rule.

50

Breathe in. One, two, three. I swallow hard. The lump in my throat shrinks from supersized meatball to frozen green pea.

What an idiot.

Me, I mean.

I can't believe I thought that Weird Nobody Nothing was worth a good deed.

Seventh Grade Social Studies

I race down the hall, barrel through the door into Social Studies, and sit at my desk. We're studying the Teapot Dome scandal, which, at this particular moment, strikes me as the most fascinating event in human history since the invention of chocolate.

Mr. Bergstrom, our Social Studies teacher, puts on his reading glasses and hunches so far over his textbook that all we see is the three-strand comb-over across his bald head. He always reads in a monotone whisper to make up for the fact that he's nearly deaf and afraid of talking too loud.

I want to concentrate, to think about something else after what just happened with Weird Bobby, but Mr. Bergstrom's words dissolve between air molecules before they reach my ears. In about ten seconds, I'm in major daydream mode as every thought bubble passing through my brain pops before I can catch it.

Then I glance at Amber, and my brain jolts awake.

Amber is a world-class texting machine. She texts Genna, Maddie, and me for every second of this class, every single day. But right now, she's staring into space with the same look she had on her face when I asked at our sleepover about her family's plans for her birthday.

I shouldn't have asked. If I'd thought about it for a split second beforehand, I wouldn't have.

Because I should have known.

There are no family plans.

Ever since her sister Jessie began making "bad choices," their mom and dad barely pay attention to Amber at all. They walk around like empty shells of their former selves, as if their parental souls were sucked up by Good Child Gone Bad syndrome.

All Amber wants is for her parents to see her without their worries about Jessie blocking their view. But that's not happening so long as Jessie is living with her bad-boy, motorcycle gang boyfriend.

I never thought about how lonely Amber must be without Jessie—and with her parents totally checked out of parenthood. It's no wonder our Friday night sleepovers were her idea.

I text a smiley face to Amber, but she's still not looking at her phone. I give her a real life smile and send super-strong ESP thought vibes to make her look my way, but since we've never had ESP before, I suppose it's too much to hope that we'd be struck with the gift at this particular moment.

Maddie glances at me then points to her mouth, crosses her eyes, and whispers, "Are you okay?"

I have a hunch my frozen smile bears more than a passing resemblance to every killer clown's smile in every killer clown movie I plan to never see.

It's no use anyway. Amber's in another universe, so I start scrolling absentmindedly on my phone.

And then it hits me.

Amber needs a good deed as much as anyone I know. And I know just what that good deed should be.

We're going to make this her best birthday ever.

I text Maddie and Genna thirteen birthday cakes, *Amber Amber Amber*, and a bunch of floating hearts.

Maddie texts a question mark back right away, and I explain.

"Theme?" Maddie texts.

"Softball?" I text back.

Maddie texts four softballs, five balloons, and six smiley emoji, but Genna, who is sitting between us, still doesn't answer. I poke her with my elbow and point to my phone, but she almost never texts in school, even in this class.

Maddie and I are figuring out ideas for a birthday video for

Amber when Genna finally pokes me back and nods toward Mr. Bergstrom.

"He's called on you three times," she whispers without moving her lips.

You have got to be kidding. Mr. Bergstrom hasn't called on a single student all semester.

Not one.

"Ms. Greene?" he says, for what my deductive reasoning tells me is the fourth time.

"Can you repeat the question, please?" I say.

"Perhaps you'd care to share the urgent matter that has you fused to the phone you are not allowed to have in class?"

"No, thank you," I say, instinctively covering my phone with my hands.

Genna kicks my foot.

The air in the room sizzles.

Mr. Bergstrom waits.

I can't think of anything to say.

Just my luck. All semester long, Mr. Bergstrom hasn't looked up from his notes once. He never notices, today or any day, when the room goes silent and our eyelids are in ready, set, droop mode.

He never notices us at all.

"Class," I finally blurt, in a very loud voice so he'll hear me. "I was checking out stuff about ... um ... class."

I can almost feel Genna's body tense up as everyone in the room goes still.

Mr. Bergstrom raises an eyebrow.

I sigh. A too-loud, holy-cow-if-he-checks-my-phone-I'm-in-for-it-big-time sigh.

Luckily, I don't think Mr. Bergstrom heard me.

My brain begins to buzz, and I remember something as my synapses snap and connect. On the first day of school, Genna told us that once upon a time, Mr. Bergstrom was a crackerjack teacher who did cool projects.

I have to admit, I had my doubts when she said that. I still do, considering that Mr. Bergstrom's performance all year has not given even a miniscule hint of any former crackerjackness.

But at this moment, Genna's story is all I've got.

"The thing is, I was wondering ... maybe we could do a final project like everyone in this class used to. And when we're done, you could throw an ice cream party like you used to. It would be," I pause to think, "fun."

Everyone stares from me to Mr. Bergstrom and back again.

He closes his eyes for a moment. Then he looks at me, presses his lips into a determined line, and nods.

I don't believe this. I was only trying to save my tush from days in detention by keeping Mr. Bergstrom from seeing the not-class-related-Amber-birthday-party-planning on my phone.

But I think something just happened deep inside him.

For both our sakes, I hope it's something good.

Principal's Office, Trouble, Monday After School, A Little After 3:00 p.m.

"Neon," Ms. Goodworthy begins, "do you know why I asked your parents to join us in my office?"

I shrug and stare out the picture window behind Ms. Goodworthy's desk to the athletic fields and the fringe of woods surrounding them. I'm pretty sure I know, but if I'm wrong, I don't want to confess to anything they may not have gotten wind of.

"We're all a little worried about you."

Yup. I was right.

At last, they're going to tell me the truth. I guess my parents needed Ms. Goodworthy to do it because it hurts too much to tell me themselves.

"I understand that today in the cafeteria, you knocked over a chair and yelled at Bobby Updegrove. Is this true?" Ms. Goodworthy asks, her stern tone cushioned by her soft Jamaican accent.

I don't answer. This isn't where I thought she was going.

"And last week, you punched Edward Rasmussen."

"But that jerk—"

Mom winces. Before Dad can start talking, Ms. Goodworthy holds up her hands.

"Now, I've explained to your parents that I didn't call them about the Edward escapade because I felt that your anger at him was justified, just not expressed as we'd like it to be. I thought you understood after we spoke that you need to redirect your feelings appropriately."

"Neon," Mom says, pulling my attention away from the baseball team congregating near home plate and Genna walking past them, looking for me. My phone vibrates. I'm late for cheerleading practice. "Dad and I are concerned that losing your temper once is an aberration, but twice ..." Worry is radiating straight out from Mom's eyes. Straight into my heart.

As her voice trails off, Dad chimes in. "Twice is a pattern. You can't go around losing your temper and hurting people."

"Is there anything you'd like to talk about, Neon?" asks Ms. Goodworthy, her narrowed eyes brimming with concern. "With your parents alone, or me, or perhaps Ms. Subcondoleez?"

The school counselor. For the messed up kids. The ones who should be messed up, anyway, whose dads are in jail or whose moms ran away with the pizza delivery guy.

They're acting like I'm nuts or something.

I take a deep breath and try to talk.

Silence.

I try again.

Nothing.

If I say it out loud, to Mom, and Dad, and Ms. Goodworthy, who must know or else why would Mom and Dad let her go on like this, if I say it out loud to them ... I told Weird Bobby because he doesn't matter. He's more like a robot than a person, anyway.

But if I say it to them

Tears

Especially to Mom

Tears — twice in one day.
 If I say it to her
Don't let them see.
It's real.
Deep breath Hold it Hold it Hold it.

I want to run away, to hide from everyone, to make it all not true. I picture myself in our cabin at the lake, where nothing ever changes. Where everything would be normal again.

Where I would be normal again.

I look at each of them and land inside Mom's worried eyes. "Everything's fine, Mom."

"You can't lose your temper that way," Mom says. "We all feel angry sometimes, but you can't take it out on other people."

"It's in your control, Neon. This is no time to start making bad choices," says Dad.

"Like Jessie Rockingham?"

"What?" Mom blinks.

"Jessie?" Dad puts on a blank look, as if Amber's big sister never crossed his mind. But when he glances at Mom, who glances at Ms. Goodworthy, shades of red, from hint-of-rose to deep burgundy, color all six of their cheeks.

"Why?" I say.

I don't say, "Why won't you tell me? Why can't I ask you?"

Mom's red cheeks go white. Dad clenches his teeth until his jaw muscles pulse, which is what he does when he's fuming — ice-in-his-veins fuming. I realize my "Why?" came out as "Why shouldn't I make as many bad choices as Jessie Rockingham?"

Ms. Goodworthy jumps in before either of my parents can say anything they'll regret.

"Neon, another outburst like the one today with Bobby Updegrove, and I'll have to consider suspending you."

Why didn't I think of that?

I haven't been giving enough thought to how I actually want to spend the twenty-two days and sixteen hours I have left on this planet. This is one of the problems with not being naturally introspective.

"You know, Ms. Goodworthy, you should probably go ahead and suspend me right now," I say, wondering if I should mention my rudeness in Mr. Bergstrom's class to seal the deal. Then I put on one of those resigned smiles that TV-show teenagers do when they get in trouble and add, "Otherwise, it might not seem fair to everyone else."

"Neon," Mom says, "that's a terrible idea. You'd fall behind in your schoolwork and you'd miss cheerleading practice—and orchestra. You love orchestra. I don't—"

Love?

I never said I love orchestra. I just never complained about going.

"Suspension is a last resort," Ms. Goodworthy says, looking at Mom and Dad. "We prefer to work difficulties out at school. Neon has always been a strong leader. She just has to learn to harness those high spirits and we'll all be back to normal." Ms. Goodworthy leans forward over her desk with a stern but understanding expression. I bet she has to use that one a lot. "How about it, Neon?"

I feel it. Mom and Dad's love and concern, and confusion. I can hardly breathe as an emotion I don't recognize—I think it may be guilt—ties invisible ribbons around my heart.

The last thing my parents need is for their dying kid to do a Dr. Jekyll and Madam Hyde.

"Sure." I nod slowly. "I'll do my best."

Jessie and Knuckles

Every grown-up in town thinks of Amber's older sister Jessie when good kids do something bad. That's because when Jessie was our age, she was just like us, as in Queen of the Cafeteria and Ruler of the Seventh Grade. Then an overdose of puberty or hormones or something hit when she turned fifteen, and she began making, as the grown-ups say, "bad choices."

Except Jessie's were World-Class, Championship Bad. She's

eighteen now and has **KNUCKLES** tattooed across her tush from here to yonder, which I know because I saw it myself when Amber, Jessie, and their mom and dad came up to our cabin in Maine for the first time in ages last summer. Jessie told Amber and me that Knuckles has *JESSIE* tattooed across his tush, too. While I'm sure Knuckles would be delighted to show us in person, we have not yet had the pleasure of seeing for ourselves.

Knuckles is Knuckles Malone, the guy Jessie lives with, and the former King of Heaven's Hellions, our local motorcycle gang. He got dethroned because he kept breaking their Code of Honor. Big Time.

According to Amber, the Heaven's Hellions' Code of Honor has three rules:

1. Help old ladies across the street. And smile when you do it so they ain't scared.

2. Don't bother no one who ain't bothered you first—unless it's a Devil Rider.

3. Beat the crap—sorry—not my word—out of the Devil Riders. And their friends.

All in all, not unreasonable rules considering that the history between the Heaven's Hellions and the Devil Riders makes the Montagues and Capulets—we read *Romeo and Juliet* last month—look like besties. Though I understand, despite punching Eddie Rasmussen who should be an exception to any anti-punching rules, that beating the ### out of other people is not the path to love, friendship, and everlasting harmony.

Anyway, according to Amber, good old Knuckles beat the ### out of anyone who looked at him funny, which to his pistachio-sized brain and watermelon-sized temper meant just about everyone. Finally, a couple of years ago, one of the ones he beat the ### out of got Knuckles arrested which resulted in his getting sent up the river for an extended vacation in the slammer.

On his first day of freedom after he got sprung, Knuckles was riding his motorcycle when he saw the sunlight shimmering in Jessie's long blonde hair as she was eating a strawberry sundae at the downtown Dairy Queen. It was love at first sight for Knuckles. I still haven't figured out what shimmering qualities Jessie saw in Knuckles that made her fall in love back.

He built a yurt so they could live together on the banks of the Muskimoot River. Jessie found this to be supremely romantic until it turned out that pistachio brain built it on the only spot along the entire river where it floods in the springtime every single year.

Maybe another semester or two of middle school would have helped him develop a critical thinking skill or two, considering that Knuckles told Amber he dropped out when he was sixteen in the seventh grade because everyone has to follow their passion in life, and school just "ain't mine."

If Knuckles is an example of following one's passion, I'm not exactly bowled over by the concept.

On the other hand, according to Amber, Knuckles is gentle as a baby bunny with Jessie. So, I figure between that and the yurt, even if he was too dense to know where to build it, there might be more to this Knuckles guy than his watermelon-sized temper and pistachio-sized brain.

At Home In My Room, Monday Evening

Dear Smush,

And that was it. Ms. Goodworthy said, "And we'll all be back to normal."

Like normal is even a possibility.

They all decided my punishment is to miss cheerleading practice for two days, which is a lame punishment if you ask me, considering the mega-weirdness with Weird Bobby that got me in trouble in the first place.

But there were two good things at school.

First, we decided to make this Amber's best birthday ever. Which, it turns out, besides being so much fun, will also be a good deed.

Second, I got busted by Mr. Bergstrom for texting Maddie about Amber's birthday, which at first was definitely not a good thing because I was in for it, big time. But then Mr. Bergstrom liked my project idea.

At least, I think he liked it. And I wasn't even going for a good deed with that one.

Except now, I have a new problem.

In Ms. Goodworthy's office, when Mom said, "But you love orchestra," a giant hammer popped into my head and kept pounding these words into my brain:

IT'S A LIE IT'S A LIE IT'S A LIE IT'S A LIE IT'S A LIE

Not once in my life have I ever lied and said I love orchestra—or playing the cello, for that matter. What I like is how Mom and Dad and Genna make such a big deal about how I'm going to be the next Yo Yo Ma.

It was never a big deal that they thought I loved the cello. It was never even a little deal.

But now that I've promised to do a Good Deed every day, do I have to untell a lie I never told—but never untold?

CHAPTER SIX

Science Class, Tuesday Morning, 10:00 a.m.
(22 days — 1,890,000 seconds — left to live)

If aliens from Galaxy X landed in our science room, the teeny green hairs on their tiny orange arms would quiver in fear. Our science teacher, Dr. Hernandez, gives extra credit for our discoveries, and the weirder, the better.

One look at the yellow ball python mounted by the window or the half-bald, stuffed bobcat growling in the corner, and those aliens would levitate their little blue bodies into their shiny red spaceships and hyperspeed to the other side of the Milky Way.

"Where's Amber?" I ask Genna and Maddie as they duck under the freeze-dried vampire bat dangling from the ceiling and sit across from me at the lab table when the bell rings. "We have to do the Freddies today." As in, clean the aquarium of our class turtles, Frederick and Fredricka, the red-eared sliders that Dr. Hernandez has had almost as long as the half-bald bobcat.

Genna bites her lower lip and fiddles with her binder as she talks. "Amber isn't here. Knuckles got arrested yesterday."

Two pairs of eyes bug out: Maddie's and mine.

The fact that Knuckles was in jail before he met Jessie felt like ancient history. It didn't seem like something that could be a part of Jessie and Amber's lives in the here and now.

"Why?" I ask.

"The police asked him to move his yurt. They were worried about his and Jessie's safety when the river floods again. Jessie told Amber that Knuckles lost it. He started screaming that the officer was invading the sanctuary he'd created for his woman. Then he socked him in the nose."

"Who socked whom?" I ask.

Maddie rolls her eyes. "This is Knuckles we're talking about. Do you honestly have to ask?"

"Jessie's using her life savings to bail him out of jail. All her birthday, babysitting, and holiday money. Their parents are furious," adds Genna.

"What about Knuckles' parents? Why don't they bail him out?" I ask.

"Knuckles is a mutant ectoplasm that fell from the cosmos. He doesn't have human parents," says Maddie. "He was raised by wolves."

"C'mon, Maddie." I shake my head. "He has a temper, for sure, but he really loves Jessie."

"And that makes what he did okay?" says Maddie. She and Genna both look at me like I'm the one who was raised by wolves.

"Poor Amber." I change the subject. "I hope we don't have to cancel her birthday sleepover this weekend."

"Seriously?" Maddie grimaces. "Amber can do whatever she wants—thank you, Jessie and Knuckles. Her parents wouldn't know one way or the other. They're lucky she's such a great kid."

"Good point," I say. "Especially since I already ordered the ice cream cake. Oreo and cookie dough with purple and orange frosting, and a photo of Amber pitching."

"I'm planning to make the cupcakes Thursday night," says Genna. "If anyone wants to come over, we can decorate them to look like softballs."

Maddie nods. "That's so cool! I'll text the party store during lunch to order balloons."

"Why don't we all go to the party store to pick them up after cheerleading practice on Friday, and we'll buy softball decorations, too," I say. "We'll tell Amber we have to go home to change and that she should meet us at your house later, Maddie."

"I'll stay with Amber so she doesn't suspect anything. You two can send me Snaps of the best decorations," says Genna.

"That's perfect," I say. "She won't figure out—"

"Neon," Dr. Hernandez interrupts, "the Freddies are waiting. Since Amber is absent today, I need another volunteer to help clean the—"

Jake jumps up, and before you can say red-eared sliders, he's standing beside the aquarium at the back of the classroom.

"Not a word," I hiss, shooting Maddie a death glare as I walk to the cabinet above the sink to grab two pairs of vinyl gloves.

"Here." I give a pair to Jake and put mine on. Frowning at the poop-covered rocks, I plunge my arms into the tank. "Yuck!"

"It's always gross," says Jake.

I pick up the Freddies one at a time and plop them into a big plastic bowl. Then we scoop the water out of the tank into the sink and use the mini-vacuum to clean the rocks, the plants, and the floating turtle island. We're facing each other as we clean the glass with scrub brushes, but Jake doesn't look at me.

I fill the aquarium with room temperature water and drop in the thermometer while Jake adds water conditioner. I tip the bowl with the Freddies over the aquarium, and they plunk in. They practically smile as they kick their striped green legs and swim across the clean tank.

I peel off my gloves, throw them away, and wash up. Then I grab lettuce from the mini-fridge and give a handful to Jake.

Fredricka swims to us, sticks out her long neck, and eats the lettuce piled on our outstretched palms. Frederick is the shy one. He only eats lettuce if we leave it on Turtle Island.

Jake clears his throat. His Adam's apple bobs up and down, up and down, up and down. "Neon?"

"Uh-huh?" I inch a lettuce leaf closer to Frederick to see if just this once, if I go slowly enough, he'll eat out of my hand.

"I wondered if—"

"Yes!"

The whole class looks at us. Jake goes beet red. Redder than beet red. I don't think there's a name for the shade of red racing from the bottom of his neck to the roots of his dark brown hair. He glances at Maddie's sort-of-boyfriend Mike, his head drooping inch by inch, until he's in total Jake giraffe mode.

"Did you see that? He did it! Frederick let me feed him the whole leaf!"

Jake nods. And keeps nodding. Droplets of sweat bead up under his bangs, across his no-name-for-that-kind-of-red forehead.

It's just plain weird the way Jake is so dorky around me. I mean, we've been friends since preschool. And he's Mr. Cool around everyone else.

"How exciting," says Dr. Hernandez. "Good job, Neon. And Jake and Frederick, too," she adds, sticking another lettuce leaf on Turtle Island as Frederick's reward. "Wash a bit more, you two, to be safe from salmonella. Then join the class to work on your science projects."

Jake clears his throat again. "Um ... Neon?"

The dispenser clicks as I pull out a paper towel and dry my hands. "Sorry. What were you saying?"

"I was wondering," he says in an unnaturally quiet voice, "if you'd like to ... um, you know ... go to the Snowflake Dance with me?"

"Sure." I crumple the paper towel and toss it in the trash. Then I remember to look at him and give a quick smile.

"Really? That's great!" As he lifts his head and straightens his shoulders, he morphs back into Cool Jake, aka the cutest-boy-in-seventh-grade-whom-everyone-else-is-in-love-with.

"That's great," he says again. "Thanks."

"Thank you for asking," I say magnanimously.

I'll bet this is exactly how Queen Elizabeth felt when she bestowed a royal honor on one of her subjects.

Magnanimous.

I like that word. Magnanimous. Generous, charitable, big-hearted. We learned it for the vocab test last week.

Tuesday Night, My Room

Dear Smush,

Genna was right about the head drooping like a lovesick giraffe thing. As soon as I said "Yes," Jake stood taller, and when he did, his tangle of rubber arms and too-long legs looked almost like his sixth-grade, cuddly self. Or would have if that Adam's apple of his had stopped bobbing up and down for one measly second.

It's not that Jake annoys me.

It's just, when I look at him, I feel nothing.

Okay. Not nothing.

Once in a purple moon, my maybe-he's-still-cute-after-all feelings bubble up for a minute or two. Or three.

But mostly when I look at him, the feeling I get is, "What happened? You used to be cute. Now you're a human apple-bobbing machine."

The truth is, I'm going to the **Snowflake Dance** with Jake as a good deed.

I'm not looking forward to dancing the Minuet, or whatever kind of dancing Ms. Goodworthy will actually let us do, for three hours of total awkwardness with whichever Jake shows up—Lovesick Jake, whose eyes will be Krazy Glued to me like magnets, Dorky Jake, in droopy giraffe mode, or Cool Jake, who might at least talk to me.

Maybe if we dance all night, I'll finally figure out what everyone else sees in him. And considering that I'm the only seventh-grade girl not in love with him, maybe I'll finally figure out why Jake's still stuck on me.

CHAPTER SEVEN

Media Center During Homeroom, Wednesday Morning, 8:15 a.m. (21 days — 1,809,900 seconds — left to live)

"Neon?"

Oh, no. No, no, no.

Every time I've seen Ms. Petrie since lunchtime last Wednesday, I've hightailed it in the opposite direction. I know what she wants. And I don't want to do it.

"Hi, Ms. Petrie." I step on it, hoping she won't notice that I'm walking toward the librarian's desk as fast as I can.

"You were a natural with Angel last week," she says.

"I think I freaked her out." I shrug, as Ms. Kaplan, the librarian, checks out *The History of Voting in America* for our group's Social Studies project. I've already learned that for most Americans, getting the right to vote — and keeping it — wasn't exactly a piece of cake, unless you happened to be a white, Christian, land-owning man.

I open the book and frown to make it look like I'm concentrating, but Ms. Petrie doesn't take the hint.

"It was a tough situation, but you handled it well. You'd be great with the kids in the Friends and Buddies Club," Ms. Petrie says, giving me a seriously intense *You can do it, Neon,* look.

"Thanks," I say, not happy at how this is going.

"We're going bowling on Friday. We could use a few more volunteers."

I try to answer. Except nothing pops out of my mouth.

I've been working on my excuses ever since Ms. Petrie told Genna to tell me that Angel's been wearing my pink sweatshirt every day, but the only thing popping into my brain is the truth: Angel seems like a nice kid, but this dying girl already tried twice with one weird kid, aka Weird Bobby, and it was two big wastes of time.

Time being something I don't have to waste these days.

"Just think about it." Ms. Petrie smiles, leaving me at the check-out desk.

"I will," I say. Which would have been a total lie in the past.

It's not a total lie now because, honestly, I'm a little conflicted.

I want to spend the time I have left with my friends. The problem is, I signed up for doing a good deed a day.

Do I get to choose the good deeds?

Or do the good deeds choose me?

Wednesday Morning, English Class

"Good morning, super scholars!" Mr. Martin, my favorite teacher, paces back and forth as we rush into the classroom.

Posters of the covers of books we've read so far this year—*To Kill a Mockingbird, Wonder, The Diary of Anne Frank, Lily's Crossing*—are lined up on the wall behind him. We scramble into our seats, shoving phones into our backpacks and pulling out laptops, notebooks, paper and pens—except Weird Bobby, who's sitting alone at one of the class computers staring at the screen as we walk in.

"For today's free-write," Mr. Martin says, flinging his right arm out. Amber ducks as his elbow whizzes past her head, the static electricity making her long blonde hair fan out like a peacock's tail as he continues, "I'd like you to reflect upon your lives."

We slink lower in our seats as Mr. Martin walks faster and faster between the rows.

"Imagine. You're one hundred years old. Did your dreams come true? Did they change as you grew older?"

Fling to the left.

"What were your most difficult and your happiest moments?"

Double fling to the right.

Maddie, Genna, and I glance at each other. Amber stayed at Genna's last night. This is definitely not one of her happiest moments.

"Were you a generous spirit or a selfish soul?"

Fling up, fling down. Fling left, fling right.

And repeat.

"You have fifteen minutes."

He collapses, exhausted and satisfied, into the chair behind his desk.

And we have fifteen whole minutes to reflect upon our made-up hundred-year-long lives. That's Seventh Grade English for you.

I hold my pen and begin. I think better when I start writing on paper instead of the computer because of all my writing in Smush.

My name is Neon Blue Greene. Today is my one hundredth birthday, which makes me a very old lady.

The hardest moment in my life was whe

My hand stops mid-e.

I was writing just like always. As if everything is okay, and I'm a normal kid who has as much chance as any other kid of growing up to be one hundred years old.

Except I'm not a normal kid. Not anymore.

I cross out that sentence and begin again.

My dreams did not come true because I died when I was twelve years old.

The hardest moment of my life is right now in this class because of this stupid assignment and because I have no idea how or why I'm dying. My parents won't talk to me about it, and whenever I'm about to ask, my brain implodes into a black hole of terror, and my heart shatters into a million tiny pieces, and—

A wave of nausea rises from the bottom of my stomach, smashing into the tsunami of pain crashing down from the top. I bolt out of my seat, grabbing my paper so no one sees it.

"Mr. Martin?" I cross my arms and press against my stomach. "Sick. Emergency."

He knits his fuzzy eyebrows together as he stuffs an orange girls' bathroom pass into my hand. "Do you need someone? The nurse?"

I shake my head and race out the door.

"Neon!" Genna hurries after me.

Amber follows her as Maddie asks, "What's wrong?"

I wave them back, jog down the hall, and turn the corner. The storm in my digestive system whooshes up and up, into my throat. I bang open the bathroom door, rush into a stall, bend over the toilet. And puke.

My shoulders shudder. My body is covered in sweat.

The smell in the bathroom—a mix of everything bathroom, and my puke, and Jordan's infamous B.O. lingering in the air—is making me nauseous all over again.

I wipe my mouth with toilet tissue and smell my armpits. It's not Jordan's B.O. It's mine.

I grab a bunch of drab brown paper towels, drench one with cold water—since that's all there is in this bathroom—and soap. From a full soap dispenser. Now that's what I call a miracle.

I lift my shirt and wash under my arms. I figure no one's likely to walk in here in the middle of class. Though right now, I couldn't care less. I wet my hands and smooth my hair. Then I gargle with water and some of that soap.

Oh, great.

Now I'm foaming at the mouth. I've added poisoning myself with liquid soap to whatever else is killing me.

I rinse—and keep rinsing—until the soap bubbles go away and my taste buds are coated with the rusty, metallic flavor of Wilson-Pike Middle School bathroom water.

I check myself in the mirror over the sink. My face is pale. My hair is flat and damp. Not my best fashion-forward look, but not much different from when I shower after gym class.

My legs begin to wobble as I walk into the hall. I slide down the wall, bumpety bumping my spine down the yellow cinder blocks until I'm squatting with my arms around my knees and my head resting in my arms.

Those words.

Those words on the paper looked—felt—so real.

A shadow spreads across the floor. Something is blocking the sun streaming from the small rectangular window above the orange lockers.

Weird Bobby.

He's standing in front of me, staring straight ahead and doing that one, two, three, four, five twisty thing with his fingers.

"What are you doing here?" I say. "You'll get in trouble."

He sticks out his other arm. There's a red boys' hall pass clutched in his grimy fist.

"Where'd you get that?"

His words tumble out in a crush. "I said I had to go to the bathroom."

"But you never lie. You don't know how."

"I do have to go ... to the bathroom," he says.

"Oh. Better hurry then."

"Genna said," and he continues in a perfect imitation of Genna's voice, "'Something's not right with Neon. I'm worried.'"

"People get sick," I say.

"Genna is smart," he says.

"Your point?"

"You said you ... don't want people to know. If you don't go back to class, Genna will know." Without glancing at me once, he turns. "I'm going to the bathroom now."

"Live it up," I say.

He heads toward the boys' bathroom, his sneakers squeaking across the gray-and-white-flecked linoleum floor.

I take a deep breath and check the hall clock. Seven and a half minutes until the second period bell. I close my eyes and rest my head against the cinder block wall.

And wait.

The weird thing is I feel fine. Okay, not right this second, but that's only because of Mr. Martin, my formerly favorite teacher, and his stupid assignment.

Although ... I did have a headache on Monday after my visit to Ms. Goodworthy's office. Now that I think about it, I had a bad headache during orchestra a couple of weeks ago, too. And there was that whole nauseous and dizzy thing during our Friday night sleepover at Maddie's house.

Maybe I haven't been feeling as fine as I thought.

I pull out my phone and search headache, dizzy, nauseous.

Flu, vertigo, virus ... brain tumor.

Genna's grandpa had a brain tumor. He had to have an operation and chemotherapy. He didn't remember things as well as he used to after all that, but he was pretty okay otherwise for a few years. Then he wasn't. He was one of the nicest grandpas ever, too.

I must have the other type of brain tumor. The kill-me-in-less-than-a-month type of brain tumor.

I expect that any day now I'll lose consciousness.

Unless I just fade away.

I wonder if coughing is a sign of a brain tumor. Sometimes I cough when I wake up in the morning.

Searching cough. Cold, flu, asthma ... tuberculosis.

A brain tumor and tuberculosis.

No wonder my parents can't tell me. It's like their daughter has turned into the medical combo platter at Captain Nielson's, except instead of surf and turf, I have TumorTuber disease.

I'll bet I'm unique in medical history.

I could donate my body to science. I'd be a perfect specimen for scientists to study—for someone with untreated TumorTuber disease, anyway. That should count as dozens of days of good deeds. It sure would take some pressure off the good deed doing.

Hold on.

If I get my Miracle, I'll be alive. I won't have a body to donate to science.

New deal.

If I get my Miracle, I'll donate my body to science later.

Really, really later. When I die of old age. In my sleep. With my dozens of children, grandchildren, and great-grandchildren all around me. And I'll be over a hundred years old, like in that stupid English assignment. And I'll have a famous career as—I don't know as what yet, but it will be great, and—

I take a breath.

Slow down.

I need one Miracle. One very specific Miracle.

And if I get it, I promise to donate my body to science when I die.

Period.

That should count for something.

After School, Wednesday, Weird Bobby #3, As In Third Time's The Charm?

Weird Bobby is sitting under a maple tree next to the basketball court as I'm leaving school after orchestra. Mike, Tommy, Sarah, and a bunch of other kids are playing HORSE. Weird Bobby's not watching.

"Waiting for someone?" I ask.

Mike turns around so his back is facing the goal. Closing his eyes, he tosses the ball over his shoulder from the foul line. Swish! The ball glides through the net.

Everyone shouts and high-fives him.

Everyone except Weird Bobby, who keeps looking sideways. And not answering me.

"If you don't have plans, you might as well come with me to my neighbor's house. It wouldn't hurt you to do a good deed for a change."

Why did I say that? I'm done with Weird Bobby.

Before I can say, "Never mind," he stands up, swings his backpack around his shoulders, and sticks his arms through the straps so smoothly I figure he must spend all his spare time practicing.

"Where's your cello?" he asks, his eyes fixed on the maple tree.

"The instrument closet."

"You're in orchestra. Don't you have to practice?"

I shrug. "I take it home on weekends sometimes," I say, and start walking before I fall into the deep pit of cello guilt all over again. I turn back to Weird Bobby who hasn't moved. "If you're coming, now's the time."

He follows me across Washington Street and past the baseball field, as we start the four-block trek to my house. Clutching his head with one hand and knitting his mousy-brown eyebrows together, he laser-focuses on the sidewalk. Then he begins to chant, in his own voice, without stammering,

Step on a crack, Break your mother's back.
Step on a line, Break your father's spine.
Step on a crack, Break your mother's back.
Step on a line, Break your father's —

"Hey," I yell. "Cut it out!"

Weird Bobby doesn't answer. He's too busy stepping, hopping, and jumping over every jagged crack, invisible line, and gnarled tree root busting through the concrete to hear me.

If he doesn't stop that monotone chant, my head is going to explode.

He pivots to avoid the trash cans on the sidewalk in front of Mr. DelMonico's house, loses his footing, and crashes into my ribs.

"Ow!" I cry.

"Sorry," he says, but he doesn't look up. He zooms in on a dandelion sprouting from a ribbon of dirt in the pockmarked cement.

Somehow or other, Weird Bobby makes it to my house without breaking his mother's back, his father's spine, or anyone else's bodily parts—most especially mine.

"Come on in." I leap up the three steps to our back porch. "We have to get Rainbow."

He stops short and freezes a few feet from our kitchen door, his arms plastered against his sides like he's about to drill straight down into the ground.

He shakes his head.

I think.

Not a single strand of his greasy brown hair so much as

flutters, which makes it hard to tell if this human impersonating a frozen hydraulic drill is shaking his head.

Rainbow runs over when I open the door. I bend down so she can lick my face hello, but she rushes past to go outside.

She circles Weird Bobby once, plunks herself next to him, and tilts her head, her brown eyes looking at him with an expression I don't recognize. Not Love-Me-Feed-Me-Pet-Me eyes. Not Think-Neon-Think Wise-Dog eyes.

They look like Patient-Dog eyes.

Weird Bobby's right hand levitates upward until it's parallel to the ground, though his wrist is still glued to the blue jeans covering his thighs.

Rainbow scoots on her rear one centimeter at a time until she's scooted her head under his hand.

It's a standoff.

Patient Dog versus Weird Bobby.

Weird Bobby blinks. Then he snatches his hand from Rainbow's head and sticks it under his left arm.

"Let's go," I command, and Rainbow bounces behind me.

Step on a crack, Break your mother's back.

My spine prickles with annoyance as Weird Bobby begins his head-exploding chant all over again, sliding and squirming on the short walk to Mrs. Valentine's white picket fence. As I open the gate and crunch down the pebble path, I remind myself that exploding at the weirdest boy in school is not my path to a miracle.

"Hello, Neon dear," Mrs. Valentine says, opening the midnight blue front door as Rainbow clomps past her, straight to the kitchen. "Bobby! What a nice surprise."

Mrs. Valentine smiles, her gray curls springing free as she takes off her crimson and navy Huskies cap. "How are you both? I haven't seen you at the pool lately, Bobby. Everything okay?"

I didn't realize I was frowning until Mrs. Valentine adds, "We're old friends from open swim at the YMCA."

"I had swimmer's ear." Weird Bobby looks down, fixing his

gaze on a yellow and orange rectangle in the geometric pattern on Mrs. Valentine's new living room rug.

"I'm very sorry to hear that."

It's quiet for a moment. It feels strange with Weird Bobby here. For the first time in my entire life, I'm not sure what to say to Mrs. Valentine. Rainbow, on the other hand, isn't feeling awkward at all as she circles back and gives Mrs. Valentine her Love-Me-Feed-Me-Pet-Me look.

"C'mon, kids. I think this puppy needs a snack. I'll bet you do, too."

We follow Mrs. Valentine to the kitchen and sit. She scrubs the dirt off her hands at the kitchen sink. Then she brings a pitcher of milk and a platter of chocolate chip cookies to the table, warms the banana bread Mom made, and sets out plates and glasses.

Rainbow bats at the silver dog bowl Mrs. Valentine keeps just for her.

"Rainbow," I scold. "That dog sure takes liberties."

"Don't you worry," Mrs. Valentine says as she chops some chicken livers. "You know I can't resist this scoundrel." Petting Rainbow, she fills the bowl and sits down with us.

"Yum," I say, as the sweet, chocolatey taste of warm cookie melts in my mouth.

"Where did you grow up?" A squeaky voice drifts through the air. Weird Bobby is looking at Mrs. Valentine. Right at her. Then he turns bright red and studies his milk as if it's a life form from another solar system.

"I was born in Brooklyn, New York. So was Mr. Valentine. We were kindergarten sweethearts." Her gray eyes sparkle and go dim at the same time. "My father was a traveling mind reader, in Coney Island, and carnivals, and such."

"He could read minds?" I ask.

Weird Bobby's mouth twitches at something in my tone. An edge, maybe, or a little creak. That kid doesn't miss a trick when it comes to his Weird Bobby way of knowing what other kids are going to say before they say it.

76

I ignore him as I continue. "Did you inherit it? The mind-reading thing?"

She laughs. "There's no such thing, dear. It was all an act. My father died when I was ten, so my mother, younger brother, and I went to live with my grandparents on their farm upstate."

"Did you ever see Mr. Valentine again?"

Weird Bobby, without looking up from the most fascinating glass of milk on the planet, shakes his head as if I've broken the world. "Neeeeon. Stupid question. They got married."

"I know." I give him an annoyed glance and turn to Mrs. Valentine. "What I meant was, since you didn't have texting or Snapchat or Instagram or anything, how did you ever meet again?"

"It was long before dinosaurs roamed the earth, as I recall, but we had our ways. Back then we had something called the telephone. And a secret weapon, too."

"Secret weapon?" I lean forward. "What was it?"

"Letters." She coughs. "We fell in love through our letters."

"Are your allergies bothering you?" I ask.

"Could be." She gives a half smile. "Or my little touch of emphysema, probably from the permanent cloud of smoke we lived in. Mr. Valentine would have smoked in his sleep, if I'd let him."

"Is that how he died?" I ask. "From cigarettes?"

"He likely would have, but he didn't live long enough to. He drove a moving truck. There was an accident."

I feel a blush burn its way up my neck to my cheeks and across my forehead. "I didn't know. I'm sorry."

Because no one—like, say, my parents—ever told me. Mom says I'm too blunt, just like my Great-aunt Evelyn. But if she'd ever told me about Mr. Valentine, I'd never have asked such a stupid question.

"Neon, dear heart," Mrs. Valentine's voice is soft, "I've known you ever since I moved next door when you were a newborn baby. You can ask me anything you want to know."

Anything.

It's like she's opened the floodgates as a million questions rush through my mind.

Why don't I think Jake Carlisle is cute anymore when everyone else still does?

Why didn't you ever have children? I know you like them since you're always nice to me, and I'm not exactly a nicey-nicey kind of kid.

How will I decide what to be when I grow up? Genna already knows she's becoming a psychiatrist, an astrophysicist, or a history professor. I, on the other hand, have no idea what I want to be —

Oh.

Right.

I can cross that worry off my list.

Well, finally. An upside to this dying thing.

A glass half full.

Lemonade out of lemons.

And all those other worthless sayings.

My eyes begin to sting, but I am not about to break my never-cry-in-front-of-anyone rule.

Especially not Weird Bobby.

Mrs. Valentine pretends she's taking a regular old bite of banana bread. From the way she's studying me, I'm not so sure her father's mind reading trick was just an act, but I can't stop one more question from crashing through my mind.

DID MY PARENTS TELL YOU THAT I'M GOING TO DIE?

I grab another cookie and gulp my milk to cover up all the gulping I'm doing to hold in my tears.

What if Mrs. Valentine does know? What if my life is like *The Truman Show*, that creepy old movie Dad always watches, and everyone knows everything about me—except me?

Okay, Neon.

Dial it back.

"Rainbow looks tired," Mrs. Valentine says, watching her walk toward the table.

Smooth change of subject. Very subtle. Unlike me.

"She does, Neon," Weird Bobby adds. "She looks tired."

"I'm a bit tired, myself." Mrs. Valentine yawns. "Neon dear, could you grab her a treat?"

I go to the cupboard and get a peanut butter dog treat. "Here, girl." Rainbow snatches it, wagging her tail as if a general just ordered, "Look sharp!"

"That's more like our Rainbow," says Mrs. Valentine.

I stand and grab Rainbow's collar. "Thanks so much, Mrs. Valentine. I'd better be going."

Weird Bobby jumps up and trips, knocking over Rainbow's metal bowl. It clatters against the ceramic tile floor in the kitchen. "Thanks so much, Mrs. Valentine. I'd better be going," he says— in my voice.

Because he doesn't know what to say.

He's not the only one.

I have no idea if Mrs. Valentine knows, and I don't know how to ask her.

I hurry to pick up Rainbow's bowl, rush out the door, and walk down the pebble path. Rainbow chases a chipmunk through the grass until it disappears into the hollow of the weeping cherry tree in Mrs. Valentine's front yard.

"Hey," I call, running after Weird Bobby, who is farther down the path ahead of me. "I have an idea. How about if you take my place visiting Mrs. Valentine when I die?"

"No." He focuses on the silken threads of a spider web floating between the rusty hinges of the wooden gate.

"Why not? I thought you were friends."

Rainbow looks at Weird Bobby with Patient-Dog eyes. We both wait. He doesn't answer.

"You like her snacks, don't you?" I say.

"What about your brother?" he finally says. "He can visit her."

"Of course he'll visit her," I say. "The Dweeb loves Mrs. Valentine as much as I do. But she needs someone whose idea of conversation is a little more sophisticated than burping the National Anthem in pig Latin."

"I don't have a chart for Mrs. Valentine. I'm not a good talker without a chart."

"You know," I nod slowly, remembering the chart he pulled out in the cafeteria, "on second thought, I don't think Mrs. Valentine needs a good talker. I think she needs a good listener."

Weird Bobby's eyes don't move. That must be the most mesmerizing spider web ever spun.

"It wouldn't kill you to do a good deed, you know. Besides, you're not the worst listener."

Rainbow scoots next to Weird Bobby, looks at him with her tongue hanging out of her mouth, and sits.

We wait.

And wait.

Rainbow may be showing a heretofore unrevealed gift for patience, but waiting for Weird Bobby to talk is trying mine.

"Go." I finally wave him away. "Just go."

He pushes the gate open, taking his time to walk through it. Then he twists and turns to avoid every crack and line as he jumps and hops and chants his way home.

Wednesday Night, My Room

Dear Smush,

Today, I realized how much I've been missing for all these years about Mrs. Valentine.

All this time, I thought I was her friend. But what kind of friend knows nothing about her life when she's always been so interested in mine?

And all it took was one question.

"Where did you grow up?" Weird Bobby asked.

Weird Bobby!

It was like he waved the green flag at the start of the Indy 500— SWOOSH!

And she's off!

Telling story after story.

About her father, the mind reader.

And how, when he died, they moved from Brooklyn to her

grandparents' farm.

About Mr. Valentine.

And how, when he died, she joined the Peace Corps to teach math at a girls' school in Ghana and stayed and stayed until she'd taught the grief right out of her heart.

Then she came back to America and moved next door to us.

All this time, I thought she'd lived next door forever.

But, it turns out, it's only been **my** forever.

CHAPTER EIGHT

Shopping After Cheerleading Practice, Thursday, 4:30 p.m.
(20 days — 1,693,800 seconds — left to live)

"How's this?" Amber twirls in a ruffled, turquoise mini dress. "With black tights?"

"No tights. It's May," Maddie says, holding up a black spandex dress and checking herself out in the mirror.

"And your black ankle boots," Genna says at the same time.

"Or I could wear my silver, strappy sandals. They have higher heels," Amber says.

"That so-called dress is too old, too tight, and too short for you, Maddie." Genna takes the spandex sliver of cloth from her and hangs it on the rack.

"It's a great dress, Amber," I say. My head is pounding in time to the music-to-go-deaf-by playing in the store. They turn it up when kids our age walk in, but I've never been sure if it's to keep us here or chase us out. "And it makes your eyes look a really cool sea blue."

"What about you, Neon? What are you wearing to the Snowflake Dance for your date with Lover Boy Jay-ake?" Maddie asks, then grabs Amber and fake kisses her.

With sound effects.

Smooch Smack Smoochie Smoochie Smooch

"It's not a date," I say.

"Right," says Amber. "It's a hippopotamus."

Maddie flutters her thick dark eyelashes at me. "I'd go to the dance with Jake in a heartbeat."

"What about Mike? Aren't you going with—"

"So would every other girl in seventh grade," Genna interrupts me.

"That's why Jake likes her." Amber looks at Genna and

Maddie. "She's unattainable. Men always like women they can't have."

"How do you know?" I ask.

"My sister."

Silence.

Even the music stops.

We never talk about Amber's sister. At least, not to Amber. Especially now that Knuckles is back in jail.

"I know." Amber frowns and scrunches her mouth to one side. "She's not exactly Sister Role Model of the Year, but she's smart about stuff. She wants to be a psychologist."

"Good. Then she can help her psycho-convict boyfriend," Maddie says, browsing through the party dresses.

"Maddie!" Genna fixes her liquid-chocolate eyes on her, but they're not looking warm and cozy.

"It's okay, Genna," says Amber. "Maddie's right. Knuckles helped Jessie find her purpose in life."

"Anyway, Jake's been in love with Neon since they were three years old and best friends in preschool," says Genna, "before she became unattainable."

"Neon's always been unattainable. Even in preschool," says Maddie.

"Even before preschool," says Amber. "Unattainable."

"He's not, I'm not, and stop talking about me like I'm not here. I'm going to the dance, aren't I? Besides, Jake has not always been in love with me. He was in love with Judy Sanchez for all of fifth grade."

"No way," says Genna. "He liked her. He loves you."

I roll my eyes—and I don't give a hint that it kind of bugged me when he liked Judy.

"Date or hippopotamus, you still need a dress," says Maddie. "Unless you already know what you're wearing."

Genna waggles a gold-sequined, super-micro mini in my face. "How about this? Right up Maddie's alley."

Amber snorts. Luckily there's no chocolate milk within a

hundred yards of those gold sequins or that would've been one expensive nose fart.

"Or this."

Maddie is holding a peach chiffon dress with three-quarter-length sleeves, tiny white embroidered flowers, and a wide, white satin sash around the waist. Its scoop neck dips a bit more in back, and the built-in petticoat makes the skirt flounce out, but not so much that it looks stupid.

It's gorgeous. And it's ... me. I can't believe Maddie's the one who chose it.

"You could wear my silver, strappy heels and be as tall as Jake," says Amber.

"But what would you wear?" I ask.

She waves her hand. "I'll dig up some shoes from Jessie's closet. She won't care."

I'm not sure what to say. It's not like Amber to talk about Jessie at all, let alone twice in one conversation, but Genna saves me.

"Go, go, go!" She pushes me toward the dressing room.

I come out a couple of minutes later and twirl around. "Buttons, please."

Genna circles me slowly, shaking her head. "If Jake Carlisle thought he was in love with you before, he's a goner now."

"Don't be ridiculous," I say.

Stepping on the small, carpeted platform, I examine myself in the full length three-way mirror. My light brown hair looks all shiny and swingy when I move, like Maddie's black hair does. My green eyes shimmer and sparkle, like Genna's brown eyes do.

This dress is magic.

Or it could be the soft lighting in the dressing room.

Either way, I love it.

"Thanks, Maddie." I smile. "It's perfect."

***

"I know something's going on, Neez." Genna stops walking as

we turn the corner to my block.

"Like what?" I carefully hang my dress bag on a low bough of a tall oak tree. With both hands, I press on the rock wall and push myself up to stand on it.

"Nice try." She aims those lie detector eyes at me, but I've been best friends with Genna for way too long to get zinged by their truth serum powers.

"I asked Weird Bobby what you guys talk about all the time. Considering that he barely talks to anyone at all, I'd bet it's you doing all the talking."

I pretend I'm only half listening as I leap to the sidewalk. Then I pull myself up on the wall, jump down, and pull myself up, again and again.

"Weird Bobby said, and I quote, 'Neon said it's a secret.'"

"He's such a weirdo." I flip my hand in the air in that dismissive, "who-even-thinks-about-him-anyhow?" way.

"If he's such a weird-o, why have you been spending so much time with him?"

"I haven't!"

"You have so."

She sits on the wall to block me. I stop short and jump to the sidewalk.

"You've been eating lunch with him practically every day. I saw you walking home with him yesterday, too."

"Yesterday?"

"I was in the car with Mom. We drove by. You didn't even notice."

Lunch practically every day? That can't be right.

But then I think. The first time I sat with him, it was to do a good deed, but it turned into a disaster. So why did I go back?

"Are you moving?" Genna blurts, saving me from some hard introspection, as if there's such a thing in my world as easy introspection.

"No!"

"There must be some reason you're missing school tomorrow

to go to the lake on a random weekend in May. Your family never does that. And you always bring friends. Always." Her voice catches for a second before she bites her lower lip and shakes her head.

Like she's shaking away hurt feelings.

"My parents want some family time." I shrug. "I don't know why we can't bring friends," I add, even though I do know. At least, I think I do. "I'm sorry we have to wait to do Amber's birthday sleepover. I already told her we'll do it next week, and I promised we'll make it an even better best birthday ever."

Genna picks up a leaf and crinkles it as she talks. "Are your parents getting divorced or something?"

Or something. You got that right.

But I raise my eyebrows to give her what I hope is an innocent look.

"Then what?" she asks.

"I have no idea what Weird Bobby was talking about. None at all. That's why he's called Weird Bobby."

I'm not being fair to Weird Bobby. And I'm lying. Which isn't part of my getting-a-Miracle-in-twenty-eight-days-or-less plan.

But it wasn't fair of Weird Bobby to say, "It's a secret," in the first place. Everyone knows if you whisper, hint, or in any way imply that you have a secret, you're begging to be begged to spill it.

Though I suppose a guy who has to write a chart for small talk wouldn't know the rules of secret keeping. I guess I should be happy that he didn't blab the whole thing.

"And what about Jake? It's like you're only excited about your new dress. You don't seem excited about the dance at all, and we've looked forward to it forever. I get that you're not in love with Jake, but you're acting ... you're acting so weird."

A sad-worried-sorry look whispers across my face. I chase it away, but Genna glimpses it before it evaporates.

"Not Weird Bobby weird, Neon," Genna says with a softness meant to soothe my feelings and dry the silent tears that only she would know are pooling behind my eyes. "It's not what I meant. I meant to say you're not yourself. I know something's wrong, Neez. I wish ... I just wish you could tell me."

It takes me a second too long to figure out what to say. "It's nothing, Genna. There's nothing to tell."

It's her turn now, and a sad-worried-sorry look whispers across *her* face.

"Well," she stands and says, "have fun at the lake."

I feel an invisible wall growing between us, as solid and strong as the rock wall Genna was sitting on. She turns and starts down the street without looking back or waving or anything.

I see the hurt in every step she takes.

A hurt that's all because of me.

CHAPTER NINE

Friday Late Afternoon At The Lake, 5:30 p.m.
(19 days — 1,603,800 seconds — left to live)

The drive to the lake feels like forever. The Dweeb and Rainbow sleep for practically the whole trip, but every time I close my eyes, Genna's face — the hurt look on her face — flashes into my brain.

Finally, we turn off the highway. There hasn't been much rain this spring, so the dirt road is dusty and dry. We drive as far as the patch of road where the rocks are too big to go over or around, and we park in the scrubby grass.

Grabbing our backpacks, we start hiking through the woods to the cabin, with Mom in the lead and Dad bringing up the rear. The smell of pine is in the air as last fall's dried leaves and brittle pine needles crackle beneath our feet.

The Dweeb runs across the bridge over the gulley with Rainbow at his heels. We call it a bridge, but it's really just a big old log. The gulley is only about three feet deep, but it seemed deeper than forever when I was little.

"Ahoooooooooooo," Rainbow yelps, slipping on the log.

I race toward her. Her claws are tearing against the bark with a scraping sound — *eeeeerrrrrreeeeeeeeeeecskcskcskcskeeee* — that sends shivers across my shoulders.

Then she tumbles sideways to the ground below.

"Rainbow!" I scream.

The Dweeb doubles back, bumps down the dirt wall on his tush, and lands next to Rainbow. I bump down next to them.

Rainbow's ears flop to one side. She doesn't move.

"C'mon girl," the Dweeb says.

I place my hand on her belly and press gently. She doesn't moan, so I start to feel the rest of her body to see if she's hurt anywhere else.

Dad hurries toward us and kneels by my side. He's looking at me as if I'm the one who's going to break while he gently strokes Rainbow's fur.

"Woof!" She jumps, almost knocking me over. Wagging her tail, she licks my face then scrambles up the small hill to Mom, who's standing outside the cabin.

The cabin has been in Dad's family forever. We come for two weeks every August and sometimes for a week in July. The whole cabin is only one big room. When everybody's here—all twenty-three of us humans, counting all the cousins, plus Rainbow, her dog cousins, and a kitten or two—we sleep outside in tents. There's no electricity except a solar charger for emergency cell phones, but no wifi or TV. No screens at all.

"J.B., Neon, how about a quick trip in the canoe while Dad opens the cabin?" Mom asks, walking toward us holding three fishing rods.

"Can we fish?" the Dweeb asks, throwing his arms around her.

"Sure," says Mom. "It's nearly dusk. The best time for fishing."

"I'll race you," the Dweeb calls, already halfway down the hill to the dock.

"Life vests!" Dad rushes after us. He buckles the Dweeb into his yellow life vest as Mom and I clip ours closed.

I hold the canoe steady as Rainbow leaps in. She sits in the cubby at the bow like she's Empress of the Lake while Mom begins paddling close to shore.

The wind is strong, making little waves that shlush, "Hello, hello, hello." The Dweeb digs into his backpack, opens a package of blueberry Pop Tarts, and breaks one into pieces. He announced in the car that if it's gross for people to eat worms, it's gross for fish, too. But when he tries to bait his hook, the Pop Tart crumbles right off.

"It's ... not ... working." He slaps the crumbs off his vest as his face turns red with frustration.

I slide the other Pop Tart from the package and break off a big corner. I rip the crusts off my peanut butter sandwich, squash Pop

Tart inside the soft middle, and roll it all into a ball. "Try now."

"It'll get mushy in the water." The Dweeb pouts.

"No way. The fish will gobble it up first," I say, even though I know he's right.

The fake blueberry aroma is impossible to resist, so I break off another corner and take a huge bite.

"Hey!" the Dweeb protests.

"You should be thanking me for my genius invention," I say as I chew, hoping Mom doesn't notice me finishing the Pop Tart, though the Queen of All Things Organic usually lets us eat almost anything we want at the lake.

I take an earthworm from the batch that we bought at the bait shop on the way here and put it on my hook. A squirmy, slippery earthworm whom I feel sorry for right now.

"Grrrrrrrrr," Rainbow growls quietly.

I point to miniature whitecaps and whirlpools in the water. "Rainbow always spots 'em before we do."

"Good girl, Rainbow," the Dweeb shouts.

"Shhh." Mom silently paddles toward the hungry fish. "Don't scare them away."

I cast my rod. Right away I feel a tug. "I've got something!" I begin reeling in the line.

"Me, too!" the Dweeb yelps.

My line jerks again, then goes limp as the Dweeb reels in not one, but two wriggling perch.

I guess those Pop Tarts were a hit.

After dinner—the perch, whole-wheat pasta with Marinara sauce, and roasted carrots and zucchini—we sit at the table next to the wood stove to stay warm. May nights are chilly at the lake.

I inspect my marshmallow roasting above the burning embers. It's golden brown, melted just enough. I squish it on a graham cracker, sprinkle on some semi-sweet chocolate chips, and press another graham cracker on top to make my version of a s'more. The Dweeb tries to take a bite of his two-Hershey-bar, six-marshmallow s'more, but it's so big, he has to break it apart to fit in his mouth.

I deal the cards to play one more game of UNO before bedtime. The cabin smells of cedar and pine, old ashes and fresh kindling, and the cinnamon in the oatmeal raisin cookies baking in the oven.

"Are you comfortable, honey?" Mom wraps a red, blue, and yellow wool camp blanket around my shoulders as I eat my sticky, chocolatey, marshmallow mess.

"Make her comfortable ... Make her comfortable ... Make her comfortable," flashes through my mind.

When the game is done, the Dweeb and I brush our teeth leaning over the deep, scratched-up porcelain sink. Then we climb into our wooden bunks along the log walls. Dad stokes the fire to keep it going as Mom settles into the faded, rust-colored cushions on the rocking chair.

She tells us the story of Lake Monster and Little Lost Loon, but I am only half listening as I wait.

I wait, and I wonder, if this is the moment, if that's why we're here, if Mom and Dad are going to tell me now.

I wait, and I wonder, until my eyes close, and I drift off to sleep.

CHAPTER TEN

Saturday Morning At The Lake, 11:00 a.m.
(18 days — 1,540,800 seconds — left to live)

"Neon! Are you watching?"

The Dweeb does a front flip off the dock.

I give him a double thumbs-up, then pull my purple and orange Chargers sweatshirt on over my T-shirt. The sun is hot, but the wind is freezing.

I'm sitting at the ancient picnic table under a stand of white pines at our beach. It's not a beach like ones in Hawaii I've seen pictures of, or anything like that. But there's a patch of sand that leads to the lake. And it's ours.

It's just ... I thought if we came here, everything would feel okay again, that everything would somehow go back to normal.

Except it doesn't feel — I don't feel — normal, and I don't want to be here anymore. I already missed my Friday night sleepover with Genna, Maddie, and Amber, and I can't even text to find out what they're doing without me today.

Besides, there's nothing to do. It's too windy to canoe. I don't feel like swimming in the ice-cold water, I'm too restless to read, and it's no fun playing UNO with only the Dweeb, but Mom and Dad are busy.

And it's not exactly like there are gazillions of good deeds lining up for me to do here in Hermitville.

Maybe I can save a toad.

A cloud drifts away from the sun, and I begin to sweat. I take off my sweatshirt and tie it around my shoulders.

I don't get it. Yesterday before we left, Dad mussed my hair, kissed me on the forehead, and said — for about the tenth time this week — "I think we could use some family time."

But if Mom and Dad want us all to be together, shouldn't we be talking about why we're having this meaningful family time in the first place? Last night was the perfect moment to give their dying child the bad news, if you ask me. Not that they've been asking—or telling—me anything.

"Neon! You're not watching!"

I push the rough redwood bench away from the picnic table. The sand is cool under my feet as I walk a few steps toward him.

I give the Dweeb another thumbs-up, and he somersaults into a perfect dive. The kid's turning into a good gymnast, in or out of the water.

A cold gust of wind whips across the beach. I untie my sweatshirt, pull it on, and look around our camp—at the swaying branches, at the yellow life vests tied to a scraggly white pine, at Mom's swimsuit dancing on the clothesline. I think she'd swim with the icebergs if we lived at the North Pole because I'm pretty sure she's part polar bear.

Squinting, I search for the Dweeb, but I don't see him. I wait another few seconds. Nothing.

How long has he been under? Thirty seconds? A minute? Two?

I'm supposed to be watching him. I always watch him.

"Jonathan!" I sprint across the beach to the end of the dock.

He's there, my baby brother, floating face down, about twenty feet out. His wavy hair forms a waterlogged halo around his head. His motionless back faces the sun. His arms lie limp by his sides.

My stomach lurches. My chest is so tight, I can't breathe. Without thinking, without a lifejacket or a rope, without calling for help, I dive in. Kicking frantically, I swim out to him. I flip him over and bring him to the surface of the water, then throw my left arm across his chest and try to keep his head from going under. The current, rough from the gusting winds, smacks his body into mine as I pull him toward the shore.

"Don't let him die," I cry as I drag him. "Isn't one child in our family enough?"

I start giving him mouth to mouth as soon as we're out of the water, before he's even lying flat on the beach. His arms are flailing, but I hold them down.

"Yuck!" The Dweeb turns his face away from mine and punches me with those flailing arms.

"You're alive!" I hug him against me.

He pushes me away as he jumps up, pushing so hard he ricochets and falls in the muck. "I'm so ... so ... mad ... at you!"

"Mad at me?" I yell, shivering in my soaking wet sweatshirt. "You could have drowned!"

"You ... ruined ... everything," he says through chattering teeth.

"Ruined everything? I saved you!"

He clenches his hands into angry fists. "I only needed two more seconds."

I pull off my sweatshirt, grab the green and white striped towel lying across the canoe, and throw it around my shoulders. I take a breath and look at the Dweeb. He's digging his nails into his thighs. Not a good sign. That's his first move when he's on the verge of a temper tantrum.

In a quiet voice, I say, "What are you talking about?"

"Two seconds to beat my underwater record."

"I'm sorry," I say, after a minute.

His little body is shuddering, and his lips are blue. I sit to wrap us together in the towel. Then I massage his arms to warm them up.

He sighs. He never stays mad at me for long.

But I feel awful.

And not awful.

It was so scary seeing him underwater.

Not moving. Just drifting.

Like he was drowning.

"What did you mean?" He stops, then starts again in a small voice. "What did you mean when you said, 'Isn't one child in our family enough?'"

I shrug and try to look blank.

"I heard you," he says, his jaw jutting out.

"I ... I don't know. I think I was panicking because I thought you were drowning."

"Who's dying?" He hammers each word as he shouts. "I heard you say a child in our family is dying."

"Die? No Dweeb-o. Nobody's dying. I mean, we'll all die someday. Mommy and Daddy. And Rainbow. And me. But not for a long, long time."

I see every emotion pulse behind his eyes—every bad emotion. Anxiety, worry, fear.

And hurt.

I'm getting to be a pro at that. Causing that look, that awful hurt look.

"It's okay." I try to hold him closer, but he shakes my arms off. "C'mon. Breathe with me." But I'm too late.

From somewhere deep in the Dweeb boy's soul, or maybe from deep in his belly, the rumbling begins. It starts quietly. It always does, the Dweeb's eerie wail, like the screech of a ghost train growing louder and louder as it hurls through a tunnel.

Dad comes running from the cabin, his unzipped sweatshirt billowing by his sides. Rainbow flies out ahead of him.

The Dweeb wrinkles his forehead and holds his breath, but it's no use. Once he gets going, he can't stop the explosion of tears. Rainbow circles him fast as a tornado, her tail pointed straight down and her fur standing at attention, as if it were electrified.

"What's the matter, champ?" Dad squats so they're face to face.

"Neon ..." Gasp, sob, gasp. "Neon ..." Sob, gasp, sob, gasp.

As Dad swoops him up, the Dweeb cries, "I'm going to be all alone without anyone, all by myself. Forever."

"Dweeb-o, I didn't say that. I only meant—"

Dad does his "Shush, Shush" hand motion. "Jonathan, you're not all alone. There are so many people who love you. Mommy and Daddy and—"

"You're all going to diieeeeeeeeee," he wails.

Dad gives me his "Really, Neon?" look.

96

Translation of Dad's "Really, Neon?" look: "Couldn't you try to be more sensitive for a change instead of as blunt as your Great-aunt Evelyn?"

How can Dad be angry at me? It's not fair.

Suddenly, I feel what I'll bet the Dweeb feels when his wail pours out of him. I want to cry and scream and wail, "I'm the one who's dying, and you and Mom won't talk to me about it."

Why did we even drive all the way to the lake for some "family time" if they weren't planning to talk about it?

I'm going to make them tell me.

I look at Dad again. He's carrying the Dweeb up to the cabin. My Dweeb, with his red, sandy, tear-stained cheeks.

I sit cross-legged in the cool sand. Rainbow pads over and lies down, plopping her head in my lap.

Until today, I hadn't thought about how the Dweeb is going to take it.

I can't tell him. I shouldn't have to be the one to tell him.

Normal parents would face this tragedy head on. They wouldn't be chicken to tell their only daughter that she's dying. Normal parents wouldn't be chicken to tell her little brother, either.

That's what parents are for.

Scratch that.

That's what normal parents are for.

Sunday Morning, My Bedroom, After The Lake

Dear Smush,

We went to the cabin for one night. Weird, right?

Supposedly we went for some family time, so I was sure this was it—we'd finally have THE TALK. The "Neon is dying" talk.

Nope. Not one word. Not on the drive there, not at the lake, not even on the drive home last night.

I didn't get why Mom and Dad haven't talked to me when time is ticking away.

But what I didn't get even more is why I still wasn't asking them.

Then this morning, it hit me.

Ever since I heard them talking, ever since Rainbow and I listened outside their bedroom door, it's felt like a bad dream, like I'll wake up any second. But if Mom and Dad tell me the truth—if they tell me it's real—there won't be any waking up. Not anymore.

Maybe it's sort of the same for them. Maybe they need to pretend everything's fine and it's all a bad dream just as much as I do.

Maybe, by not asking, I've been doing a good deed for them—without even knowing it—all along.

CHAPTER ELEVEN

Sunday Morning, 10:00 a.m.
(17 days — 1,458,000 seconds — left to live)

"Mom?" I call, as I walk into the kitchen.

The Dweeb is sitting at the table covering his plate with his hands to hide two huge chocolate chip cookies — Mrs. Valentine specials. Rainbow is nestled, round as a donut, in her bed in the corner.

"Where'd Mom go?"

"... onference ... ember?" he answers with his cookie-stuffed mouth.

"What about Dad?"

"... elping ... issus ... alentine ... all day."

Looks like I'm babysitting the Dweeb all day, all by myself, for the first time.

I'd forgotten Dad's helping Mrs. Valentine clean out her attic today. I know he's right next door if we need him. But I don't get it. What kind of parents abandon their dying child on a Sunday for hours and hours? Maybe it's supposed to be a good-bye bonding thing for the Dweeb and me, but how would we know since they tell us nothing?

I snatch one of the cookies from the Dweeb's plate. I break off a chunk loaded with chocolate chips and pop it in my mouth. Rainbow looks up with her Feed-Me eyes, so I throw her a chunk without chocolate chips.

"Hey!" The Dweeb reaches across the table and tries to snatch the cookie from my hand.

I shove the rest into my mouth. "You should be having Oatie-Oats for breakfast, anyway," I say with my mouth full.

"So should you." He pouts.

"I had breakfast hours ago. This is dessert. C'mon." I pull him up, and he follows me into the family room. "Let's watch *Harry*

Potter."

The Dweeb's eyes go wide. "Now? We're not allowed to until—"

"Sure, like you didn't already break a rule or two, Mr. Cookies for Breakfast," I say. "We'll do our homework later."

The Dweeb makes a beeline for the remote control. In a flash, the skulls at the beginning of *Harry Potter and the Goblet of Fire* fill the screen. Voldemort's snake Nagini slithers out of the mouth of one of them.

"I don't know if this is a good idea, J.B.," I say.

"Please? Please, please, please, please?" He bounces on his toes then dives into the La-Z-Boy loveseat.

I should say no, but I curl up next to him. *Goblet of Fire* is my favorite, and I'm feeling totally bonded with Harry considering that my alleged parents appear to care about me as much as Harry's Aunt Petunia and Uncle Vernon cared about him.

"That was too scary," the Dweeb says when the movie ends. "I like *Sorcerer's Stone* and *Chamber of Secrets* better." His arms are tight around Rainbow, who's snuggled between us.

I sigh. "You always ask to watch *Goblet of Fire* when Mom and Dad aren't here to say no. Then you always say it's too scary."

"I keep forgetting." He frowns.

I pull up my seat, push down the footrest, and hop off. "How about lunch at Gracie's? That'll chase those scares away."

"But Mom and Dad aren't home to take us, and you don't drive."

"It's only a few blocks, Dweeb-o."

"I'm not allowed to walk to Gracie's Diner alone."

"You're not alone. You're with me."

"Can I eat anything I want?"

"Yup. Anything you want." I hold two twenty dollar bills with pink Post-its stuck on. "Mom left these on the kitchen counter. No rules. Just our names on the notes." I smile as the Dweeb jumps off the loveseat and runs out the door in front of me with Rainbow beside him.

"*Hamburgers, sundaes, French fries, Coke. Hamburgers, sundaes, French fries, Coke,*" the Dweeb chants, loping down the sidewalk ahead of me and back again until we reach the diner. The smell of grilled burgers fills the air as I climb the three steps to the vestibule and pull open the door. Rainbow bounds inside, stops, and looks up hopefully.

"Sorry," I pat her head, "but you know the drill."

Rainbow's velvety-black ears flop down, and she skulks into the corner by the gumball machine.

"Hey, Neon," the Dweeb shouts, as he rushes inside. "Genna's here. With Maddie and Amber."

"Hey, J.B." Genna gives him a quick hug as he pops a few fries from her plate into his mouth and runs off.

Genna. Maddie. Amber.

At our booth.

Without me.

I'm wearing my dull-gray East Moose Woods sweatshirt.

They're wearing our purple and orange cheerleading sweaters. We wear them whenever we go out together on a Saturday morning after our Friday night sleepover.

So why are they wearing them today?

"Hi," I say.

"Hey, Neon," Maddie says, as Amber smiles.

"Hi," Genna says. "How was the lake?"

But she doesn't look at me. She pretends to be focusing on Gracie, who is delivering three hot fudge sundaes with mounds of whipped cream to their table.

"It was boring." I shrug and pause. Then I add, "I have to babysit the Dweeb today."

Maddie nods. "Yeah, we know. That's why we didn't call you."

Except they didn't know I was babysitting today because I didn't even know until this morning that I was babysitting today.

Calm down. I take a deep breath. These are my best friends. They'd never leave me out on purpose.

"Are you doing anything later? I'll probably be sprung before dinner."

Silence.

One thousand and ...

Two thousand and ...

"Not really," says Maddie. "Amber's birthday sleepover was last night. We would have waited for you to come home, but yesterday was her actual birthday."

"You had her ... sleepover?"

We always wait until we're together to celebrate our birthdays. All of us. Always.

That's lie number two, Maddie. Good thing you're not the one who's in the market for a Miracle.

I don't say anything. I don't say anything because I can't talk. A giant lump is blocking my throat.

It was bad enough that I was missing our regular Friday night sleepover, but it was my idea to make this Amber's best birthday ever. My idea to have a softball theme.

"And, you know, you've been so busy with Weird Bobby," says Amber.

Amber, who cannot tell a lie.

Genna's face tenses. She slinks lower in her seat. I'll bet she doesn't even know she's doing it.

"Neon!" the Dweeb calls from the big booth in the back of the small diner. "Come see what I made."

"I better go," I say, but the buzzing in my head is so loud, I can hardly hear my own voice. "Enjoy your sundaes."

Translation: I hope your ice cream is melted, your hot fudge is cold, and your whipped cream is spoiled.

I slide into the silver booth across the red leatherette cushion to face the Dweeb. He's adding packets of Sweet'N Low to the roof of his Smucker's Jam castle.

I look out the window. A single mallard bobs his shiny green head in and out of the pond, then floats along without a worry in the world.

On second thought, maybe that mallard's all alone because his friends ditched him, too.

I shake some salt on the table and balance the ketchup bottle on its side.

"One false move, and the Ketchup Ogre will crush your castle, Prince Dweeb-o of Sweetlandia!" I say.

"Nooooo!" He knocks my ketchup bottle down.

I am balancing it on the salt crystals again when Gracie walks up to our table.

"Hey, Neon. Hi, J.B. Nice castle you've got there." She whisks an escaped pink-and-lavender-streaked curl behind her ear. "So, what would you kids like today?"

"The burger deluxe special, with extra crispy fries and a Coke," says the Dweeb.

"Me, too," I say.

And a side of FSBs—Friends Since Birth—who aren't two-faced traitors.

Not that I care.

Our burgers and fries will be perfect.

And when we order dessert, I'm having extra hot fudge.

Sunday, After Gracie's Diner

"Rainbow, sit." She's already sitting on the sidewalk in front of the diner. I say it anyway when I give her a treat, just to remind her.

Gracie saves mistakes and leftovers for everybody's pets. Rainbow hit the jackpot today. I open the aluminum foil package and toss her two overcooked burgers and a chili dog. She scarfs them up so fast they're gone before I blink.

"C'mon, Dweeb-o. Let's go to Sam's." Sam's Candy Depot is half a block away, in the tiny shopping center on the corner with Bella's Bakery and the karate school. "If we're going to have Cozy Night, we need candy."

"Cozy Night! Again!" He squeals and races ahead chanting, "Can-dee! Can-dee! Can-dee!"

"We'll play candy hide and seek," I say, meaning I always hide the candy until we eat it so Mom doesn't freak out and feed us Brussels sprouts for dessert all week.

Rainbow and I catch the Dweeb at the crosswalk. As we wait for the light to change, I'm feeling worse and worse. I can't stop wondering what Genna, Maddie, and Amber are doing—without me—for the rest of the day.

"My ball!" A little voice interrupts my thoughts.

A two-year-old toddles off the curb, her chubby legs wobbling from side to side as she tries to chase the bright orange ball rolling into the street. I run toward her and see a dark-haired woman with the same panicked, frozen-faced expression the Dweeb has when he's startled awake.

"Megan!" The woman rushes into the street, wraps her hands around the girl's waist, and scoops her up. "Never, never, never!"

The little girl scrunches her face into a red, teary mess and wriggles in frustration. Rainbow bolts past us in a flash of black fur and captures the orange ball in her mouth as, a few feet away, a motorcycle speeds toward the intersection.

"Rainbow!" the Dweeb shouts and races after her.

"Jonathan—no!" I run into the street after him.

Screeeeeeeeeeeeeeeeeeeeeeeeeeeeeeech!

"Neon!"

Thud.

"Call an ambulance!"

"Don't move!"

"Is he conscious?"

"How's the girl?"

"Where's the dog?"

I open my eyes and try to raise my head. I'm lying in the middle of the street in front of Sam's Candy Depot, but I'm not sure how I got here. Sirens are blasting. An ambulance pulls next to the police car and the fire truck. People are everywhere, running and shouting, crossing in front of me.

I have to find Jonathan. I flatten my hands and push on the

rough pavement, but I can't get enough leverage to stand. My left wrist hurts so much I want to throw up.

"Take it easy," says a young woman wearing a navy blue uniform with a red, blue, and gold EMT patch. She's kneeling next to me, but I don't know how long she's been there. "Let's have a look at you." She circles my swelling wrist gently with her hand.

"Owwww," I moan.

"It looks broken. Are you having pain anywhere else?"

I close my eyes to concentrate. "My whole left side." I look down for the first time and see that my shirt is crumpled and torn.

"You look pretty scraped up," she says. "How about your head?"

I touch my hair. It's matted. And soaking wet. Then I look at my hand. No blood. "It hurts a little. Not a lot." I touch the left side of my forehead. "Here."

The EMT takes out a penlight. With her thumb and index finger, she holds my eyes open as she examines them. "I don't think you lost consciousness, but you took a hard fall. You were probably dazed for minute or two. My guess is that you caught yourself with your left arm and your wrist got the brunt of it."

"I was running to save my Dweeb. After that, I'm not sure what happened. Have you seen him?"

"Your ... Dweeb?"

"And Rainbow?" I can't believe I almost forgot Rainbow. "Have you seen her?"

A rush of worry flickers across the EMT's face, but her voice stays calm. "Your ... sister?"

"My brother. And my dog. I have to find them!"

"That dog? Over there? With your brother?"

Weird Bobby is lying on the ground, just a few feet from me. Rainbow is sitting next to him, licking his cheek while a gray-haired EMT examines him.

"Rainbow!"

She looks and yips a quick, quiet hello, but doesn't come to me. She looks back at Weird Bobby. I follow her eyes with mine.

Blood is trickling from his eyebrow—his split-open eyebrow—painting a fine, red line around his cheekbone, along his jaw, and down his neck.

"That's not the—not my brother. Jonathan. He's only seven. I have to find—ow!" My entire left side throbs as I press my right hand flat on the pavement and push to sit up.

"Try not to move," says the EMT. "I'll find your brother, and we have to splint your wrist. I'll be right back."

"Bobby," I call. The ground vibrates beneath me with the thump of feet racing back and forth. "Bobby?" I call louder, over the clatter of slamming car doors and the shouts of a police officer calling out instructions. "What happened?"

He doesn't answer.

"Neon!" The Dweeb crashes down next to me.

I reach and hug him with my right arm. "I was afraid," I begin, my voice shaking.

"I was on the sidewalk. I ran to the sidewalk," he says, his nose starting to run as he bursts into tears. "I'm sorry."

I wrap my arm tighter around him and let out the breath I didn't know I'd been holding. "It's okay. We're okay."

"Bobby saved Rainbow," he says between sobs. "He pushed her out of the way when Knuckles' motorcycle ...."

I try to make the Dweeb's words sink in, but my head feels stuffed with cotton balls.

I wonder for a second how the Dweeb knows that it was Knuckles driving the motorcycle. Then I hear Weird Bobby's voice in my head: *Neeeeon. Stupid question. Everyone knows Knuckles Malone.*

I look hard at Weird Bobby. I can't tell if he's breathing.

I get a bad feeling in my stomach, but it's not throw up this time. It's panic.

No, it's worse than panic.

It feels as if every muscle, every bone, every cell of my body is being zapped away and replaced.

With terror.

106

There's only terror inside me.

They lift Weird Bobby onto a stretcher that I hadn't even noticed was there.

This is all wrong.

If anyone should be on that stretcher, it's me. I'm the one who's dying.

They lift Weird Bobby's stretcher into the ambulance. I try to stand.

"Not a good idea." The EMT who'd been examining Weird Bobby lightly touches my shoulder. "How's the wrist feeling?"

"It hurts," I say.

"This will keep it still until we get some X-rays." He places my left forearm on top of a blue and orange splint and circles it with gauze. "You're next."

"Next for what?"

"You have to get checked out at the hospital, too."

"But I have to ride with him." I point to Weird Bobby in the ambulance. "He can't go alone."

Before the EMT can answer, I add, "He has issues. I'm his sister. And our little brother and Rainbow have to go with him, too."

"Rainbow?"

"Rainbow is his therapy dog."

He motions to someone behind me. Suddenly, they're both hoisting me onto a stretcher and into the ambulance next to Weird Bobby. Rainbow barks. Her front paws press on the floor of the ambulance as she tries to jump in, but she's having trouble keeping her balance.

"Rainbow, you're so heavy!" The Dweeb lets out a whoosh of air as he half pushes, half carries her in. Then he plops Rainbow at my feet and collapses on my stretcher next to her.

"Ow! Jonathan!"

He jumps off, and Rainbow shudders. She scooches up my stretcher until she's snug between Weird Bobby and me.

Then I see. Her right rear leg is hyperextended and dangling.

She must be in awful pain, but she starts licking Weird Bobby again. I figure no one's worrying about Rainbow germs because I said she's his therapy dog.

The EMT who helped me first is holding the oxygen steady over Weird Bobby's nose and mouth. There are wires coming out of his arms. He looks exactly like the Robot Boy I thought he was.

Except Robot Boy wouldn't have saved Rainbow.

I put my hand on his hand and squeeze. "You're going to be okay, Bobby."

I feel a slight squeeze back.

Or maybe it's just wishful thinking.

CHAPTER TWELVE

The Snowflake Dance, Wednesday Evening, 6:00 p.m.
(14 days — 1,170,000 seconds — left to live)

"Neon," the Dweeb hollers up the stairs. "Come quick!"

"Wha-at?"

"Come down here!"

I close my laptop and climb off my bed. Rainbow stretches and trundles off her bed, dragging her broken leg in its plaster cast.

"Wait there, girl," I say.

I walk down the hall and look down the stairs from the second-floor landing. "Dweeb-o, stop shout—"

Jake Carlisle is standing in our doorway wearing a black tuxedo and holding a white box.

I'm wearing a cast that matches Rainbow's on my broken wrist, my Wilson-Pike purple and orange flannel p.j. pants, Dad's old college T-shirt—and a very red face.

Jake opens the box. He takes something out and holds it in his hand.

It takes a few seconds to cut through the fog swirling inside my brain.

Tonight is the Snowflake Dance. That is why Jake Carlisle is standing in our doorway wearing a tuxedo and holding a corsage that I should be slipping on right now.

Jake sees me on the landing.

"Hi," I say, as his eyes widen in confusion.

Then his head droops and the corsage falls to the floor.

The Dweeb grabs it and sniffs, making a loud snort. "Wow! It smells great!" He pulls Jake inside. Then he runs up the stairs and shoves the corsage in my face. "Put it on!"

"Not now, J.B." I start down the stairs, not sure what to say. "Jake," I begin.

"It's okay," he says. "I guess with the accident and everything, I should have texted."

"I'm sorry. It's just, I've been home from school. I feel a lot better but," I nod at my wrist, "I've been pretty tired. They had to do surgery."

"You can still go, Neon," the Dweeb says.

Since when did my baby brother become Cupid Junior?

"Mom," the Dweeb calls, then rushes back to Jake. "She can go. Right, Jake?"

Jake steps further into the living room. I walk down the rest of the stairs until we're facing each other. He looks so nervous, I can almost see the question marks in his eyes. Then he smiles. He still has the same dimples that I used to think were cute before my attention became riveted on his up and down, up and down, up and down Adam's apple.

"J.B., what on earth are you shouting about?" Mom hurries into the living room and stops short. "Jake! Oh my goodness." Mom looks at his tuxedo, then at me.

She waits for a sign.

I have to give her credit. She's always been good at checking my expression to see if I want her to be Mean Mom or Nice Mom when she isn't sure what I want to do.

"Dweeb-o, talk to Jake while I'm getting ready, okay?" I say.

"She'll be down in a flash," Mom adds to Jake, following me upstairs.

I take my dress out of the closet. The light shimmers through the peach chiffon to the glowing satin underneath. Then my heart sinks. "I don't have the right shoes. Amber was going to loan me hers." I shrug and stop myself before I say that I don't think we're friends anymore.

Mom's "I know all" look flashes in her eyes, but I'm not sure what the "all" is that she knows.

"Maddie and Genna came over while you were napping today. They dropped off these." She reaches for a bag under the foot of my bed and pulls out a pair of silver, strappy sandals.

Amber's sandals that she was going to let me borrow.

"They said to tell you they're sorry for everything." This time a different look passes across Mom's face, a "what aren't you telling me?" look. "They said Amber couldn't bring the shoes herself because she was with Jessie and their parents visiting Knuckles in the hospital."

"Knuckles?" I've been so worried about Weird Bobby that I forgot about Knuckles.

"He has quite a concussion, but he's going to be okay. Apparently, Jessie makes him wear a helmet, and his helmet saved him from something much more serious," Mom says.

"Will he have to go back to jail?" I ask. "The accident wasn't his fault. And he just got out on bail."

"No one blames him for the accident. But honestly, honey, I'm not sure," Mom says, carefully working one sleeve of the dress over the cast on my left wrist and sliding my right arm through the other sleeve. "You could put in a good word for him if you'd like."

"I would," I say. "If it's okay."

Mom nods. "You'd be doing a good deed."

A good deed.

Mom pulls the dress over my head, and I look away.

Ever since the accident, I'd forgotten about the good deeds.

Well, I didn't exactly forget. I just stopped thinking about them.

And why I was doing them.

I was too upset about how much everything hurt, and what could have happened to the Dweeb and Rainbow, and what was going to happen to Weird Bobby.

Mom smooths the peach chiffon over the petticoat then buttons the tiny white lace buttons up the back. As she ties the white satin sash and helps me slip on the silver sandals, I remember one other thing.

The whole reason I was going to the dance with Jake in the first place was as a good deed. A good deed to save my life.

"Neon? Take a look."

"What?"

"Your dress, sweetie." Mom is looking at me with worry in her eyes.

I walk to the mirror, but my heart isn't in it.

Mom spins her index finger. "Twirl around." She smiles.

As I begin to turn, Rainbow woofs in approval.

"You look beautiful," Mom says.

Even in my own bedroom, this dress is magic.

"Sit." Mom pats my bed. She brushes my hair and pulls it half up. As she starts braiding, she weaves in a new white satin ribbon that matches my sash.

"Hey, fellas," Mom says to Jake and the Dweeb, who are so hypnotized by whatever they're playing on Jake's phone that they don't hear us come downstairs.

"Wow, Neon!" The Dweeb rushes up and hugs me. "You're beautiful."

"Careful," Mom scolds. "Don't get her dress dirty."

Jake doesn't move. Or blink. He just stands there, staring at me.

Mom picks up the corsage lying next to him on the couch. "Shall I do the honors?" Mom says when Jake doesn't realize that she's trying to hand it to him.

"Oh ... sure." He blushes now, turning redder and redder, as Mom slips the corsage on my right wrist. "You look really ... um ... nice."

"Picture time." Mom guides Jake so that he's next to me. "I have to get lots for Daddy. He's not going to believe he missed this to fix the floodlight in the Brady's backyard." She aims her phone at us. "Say Snowflake Dance!"

The Dweeb squishes in between Jake and me, then turns around and makes faces until we can't stop laughing.

"I guess we'd better get going," Jake says as his phone beeps.

We walk to the door and see Mr. Carlisle waiting outside in their minivan. Mom waves hello as if she's not one bit surprised

112

to see him.

***

"One two three, two two three, three two three," Ms. Goodworthy calls as she claps the beat, but there's no music playing.

We were doing fine dancing to her pre-approved rock 'n' roll oldies, though I have a hunch she's never listened to the words of those old songs because they aren't exactly G-rated.

Now we're all standing awkwardly next to our partners, except for Sarah and Tommy, who are doing one Sixties dance after another—the Twist, the Pony, the Swim—plus their own totally uncoordinated arm-flinging moves.

The rest of us are pretending to study the hundreds of silver and white snowflakes in different shapes and sizes hanging from the metal ceiling supports, nearly touching our heads. Their glittery paint sparkles as two floodlights crisscross the gym.

The music starts again. The DJ is playing—I can't believe it. This is worse than the "Minuet in G."

"Would you like to waltz?" asks Jake.

I roll my eyes. "To Kermit?"

Ms. Goodworthy is actually making the DJ play "Rainbow Connection." From the Muppets. Like we're in preschool.

Jake shrugs. "It's not jazz, like Etta James, or a classic, like 'Waltz of the Flowers,' but it's not such a bad song."

"Mmmmm." I shake my head. "I don't think so. Besides, I don't know how. My dad showed me the box step once. That's about it."

I almost add, "Who's Etta James, and how do you know anyway?" when a memory flashes through my brain. I can practically hear the jazz the Carlisles always had playing in their house when Jake and I were in preschool.

"The box step is easy," Jake interrupts my thoughts. "Your feet do the opposite of mine."

He reaches over to support the cast on my left wrist with his right arm and raises his left arm in the air. I lift my right arm, and he takes my hand.

The Box Step

Jake: Left foot forward.
Me: Right foot back.
Jake: Right foot forward to the right corner.
Me: Left foot back to the left corner.
Jake: Left foot slides to meet his right.
Me: Right foot slides to meet my left.
Jake: Right foot back.
Me: Left foot forward.
Jake: Left foot back to left corner.
Me: Right foot forward to right corner.
Jake: Right foot slides to meet his left.
Me: Left foot slides to meet my right.
And repeat.

We start slowly, but even with my broken wrist, I can do this. Jake's a good waltzer, and the box step isn't hard.

Everyone is watching us. And not only the dorky kids, the ones whose eyes are always glued to the popular kids like we've been sprinkled with magic fairy dust. I'm used to being the center of attention at school sometimes, but this is different.

We whirl across the floor until we're floating on air. It feels like forever—and as if time is flying. We dance and dance, spinning and dipping, twirling and laughing.

Just Jake and me on our own private cloud.

My Bedroom, Wednesday After The Dance

Dear Smush,
This is the biggest secret since the worst secret ever.
But this time, it's a good one. Sort of.
I am in love with Jake Carlisle.
We went to the Snowflake Dance, and it was like being with the

old Jake. The one I've known for my whole life. He's such a good dancer that, after a while, I didn't notice his Adam's apple bobbing up and down anymore.

Well, I hardly noticed, but I noticed his dimples more.

I was beginning to wonder if he only likes me because he really does think I'm unattainable, like Genna, Maddie, and Amber said.

Then he asked me to be his girlfriend.

I almost said yes. Because for the whole dance, I forgot.

It wasn't until he asked that I remembered.

I was sure my feelings were plastered all over my face, so I pushed them away as hard as I could. Then I tried to think of a way to say no that wouldn't hurt Jake's feelings. I couldn't think of anything. So, I went for the enigma routine. I looked into his eyes. Then, as mysteriously as I could, I smiled.

Except I wasn't smiling on the inside.

Finally, I love Jake Carlisle back. And I have to set him free.

CHAPTER THIRTEEN

The Hospital, Thursday After School, 4:00 p.m.
(13 days—1,090,800 seconds—left to live)

Weird Bobby's hospital room has more orange and purple balloons with matching ribbons cascading to the floor than the Wilson-Pike Middle School auditorium has for eighth grade graduation. He's sitting up in bed, and the TV is on, but the volume is turned off, so I can't tell if he's watching.

I pull my old red wagon next to him and help Rainbow scoot out. Between my broken wrist and her broken leg, we're quite a pair.

"I hope you like green balloons!" I untie the bunch floating from my wagon handle and tie them to the metal bar at the foot of his bed. "Green's your favorite color, right?"

"Thank you," he answers without looking at me, but he pets Rainbow, who snuggles her head closer.

"You have cards from every one of our teachers," I say, as I start reading the get well cards crammed together on the ledge beneath the window, "and this one's from Mrs. Valentine. I'll tell her you got it when I visit her later."

There are dozens more, squeezed into every nook and cranny. I open a humongous card with a Golden Retriever wearing swim trunks and goggles. "Wow," I say. "I know you like to swim, but you never told me you're on the swim team."

"I'm a fast swimmer," he says.

I turn to him and nod. Then I see the way his hospital gown pulls across his shoulders—his swimmer's shoulders. I never really looked at his shoulders before. I guess they were always invisible behind all of his weirdness.

Or invisible to the kind of person who only sees the weirdness.

"So," I sit in the faux-leather armchair, "I heard you had surgery on your leg. Mom said you may have to be here for a few more days. How do you feel?"

Neeeeon. Stupid question, I imagine Weird Bobby answering, as I survey him, from his scraped arms to the black stitches above his black eye. And his shiny, swollen, purplish-blue cheek. And the egg-sized bump on his forehead.

Rainbow barks. Weird Bobby helps her climb on the bed, and I give her a boost. As he leans toward her, the rumpled beige hospital blanket shifts, and I catch a glimpse of his cast. It goes all the way up his right leg, like Rainbow's does. Though in Rainbow's case, it's her right hind leg.

"Look." I point to my cast. "We could be triplets. You, Rainbow, and me."

Weird Bobby's eyes swivel to the closet door. He parks them there in staring mode.

Rainbow licks his face. He doesn't flinch. I figure that means he likes her a lot. Or else he's getting used to her. The hospital is letting Rainbow visit because the EMTs told them she's his therapy dog, and nobody told them she isn't.

"They ... gave me medicine for my headache."

"I heard it was a pretty bad concussion."

I take a fine point felt-tipped pen out of my backpack. "It's forest green, just like yours. Could I be the first to write on your cast?"

"Too ... late."

There are lots of forest green signatures already. Doctors and nurses and **Get Well Soon Kid! KNUCKLES.**

"Wow! Knuckles signed your cast? Did he come to your room?"

His eyes, which are still drilling a hole in the closet door, have a look I can't decipher. Then he starts talking so fast his words somersault out, one on top of the other.

"The nurse brought him. He was in a wheelchair. I signed his casts. On both legs."

"Wow!" I say again. "Did he say anything?"

Weird Bobby nods.

118

"What?"

He doesn't answer.

"Please, Bobby. Tell me."

He hesitates, then says, "'I am sorry that I ran over you and Rainbow.' He said that."

Knuckles? Sorry? I didn't think he was the kind of guy who apologized for anything. Ever. The accident wasn't even his fault.

And he knows Rainbow's name.

"Well, I'll be the first to sign your cast down by your ankle." I take the cap off the pen and begin drawing.

"You only called me that once before. In the ambulance after I ... got hit by the motorcycle."

I look up from my sketch of Rainbow on a motorcycle. "Called you what?"

"Just Bobby. Not Weird."

My face, arms, and legs—broken wrist included—are burning hot-tomato-red with shame. I didn't know I ever called him Weird Bobby to his face.

"You didn't." He reads my mind in his Weird Bobby way of knowing what we'll say before we say it. "But you thought it. Every time."

Except he's not Weird to me. Not anymore.

"I'm sorry," I say.

"I know," he says.

But his eyes stay focused on the closet door.

Then I remember. I shouted his name one other time—Bobby, just Bobby—after the accident when I saw the blood, when he was unconscious.

I didn't think "Weird Bobby" that time either.

Not that it makes up for the thousands of times I did.

"Why'd you run to save Rainbow?" I ask. "I was halfway across the street after her already."

I wait.

"I wasn't trying to save Rainbow. I was trying ... to save you," he says, at last.

"What?" My voice goes hoarse. "You could have been killed."

"I had to push you away from Knuckles' motorcycle." He pauses. "It was a green light. He would have hit you."

"You pushed me out of the way? That doesn't make sense. You don't do things that don't make sense. To risk your life when I'm ...." My voice catches.

Sitting here in Bobby's hospital room is so ....

I close my eyes.

So real.

"Anyway, you know what it means that you saved my life, don't you?"

He doesn't look at me or answer, but I've gotten used to talking to the side of his face and the top of his head. "It means I have to save your life in return. Or it might mean you're responsible for me forever, W.B. I forget."

His face goes pale and his shoulders squeeze together. He shifts his gaze to the tray table across his bed. This is not a happy look.

My brain crackles like a staticky TV that turned itself back on after a power blip. Bobby knows I only have two weeks left to live. And now I've made him feel as if it's his responsibility to keep me alive forever.

The shades behind his eyes go down. "W.B.," he finally says in an even more monotone voice than usual. "For Weird Bobby."

"No. No. No." I shake my head. This isn't going the way I meant it to, but before I totally blow it, I try again. "W.B. for Wonder Boy. Or Wonder Bobby? You know, like a superhero," I say, my voice and enthusiasm fading away.

"How about A.B.?" I ask, after a minute.

"A. For ... autistic?" he says.

"A for awesome!" I say.

But I wonder if that's why he's different. I start to ask, but for once, I stop myself. Because it doesn't matter. Not anymore.

Then Bobby the mind reader strikes again.

"I'm an autistic person, in case you didn't know, but Mom says my official diagnosis is Awesome Bobby because I do awesome things."

"I told you!" I say. "A.B. Awesome Bobby."

But he ignores me.

"I can't always tell what other people are feeling. Sometimes I miss ... nuances. That's what Mom says. Do you think so?"

"Maybe," I say. "A little."

"Mom says sometimes I'm too blunt."

"Blunt?" My voice rises. "I know someone like that."

"Who?"

"My Great-aunt Evelyn."

Bobby gives me a look. He might miss some nuances, but he sure catches everything else. "Anyone else?"

"Have anyone in mind?" I tease him, raising my eyebrows, but I don't think he gets it. It must be one of those nuances he misses. "Okay, okay. A few people think I'm too blunt sometimes, too. Do you think so?"

"Maybe," he says. "A little."

I burst out laughing.

Awesome Bobby, who can imitate voices like a movie star, and knows what other kids will say like a psychic, and makes lists to puzzle things out like a scientist.

And who saved Rainbow and me, like a superhero.

Whether he likes it or not.

I didn't think Bobby's eyes could look further down at his tray, but they do. And his shoulders hunch further forward than before. If he keeps this up, he can add contortionist to his talents, but I think I've made him uncomfortable enough with all this Wonder Boy, Awesome Bobby stuff.

"Don't you know, Neon?"

"Know what?"

"I made a chart."

"Can I see it? Is it as good as the chart you showed me in the cafeteria?"

"It's at home."

"Your chart's at home. Okay."

I have no idea what he's talking about. He saved me, and he saved Rainbow, but I'm beginning to wonder if that concussion brought him to a whole new level of Weird Bobbyness after all.

He frowns then quickly unfrowns as his black stitches pull. "Number One," he says. "Neon's parents love her."

"Um ... Bobby? What?" I say. But I'm thinking, how would you know?

"There." He points to the hospital menu on the tray. "Write!" His voice rises in frustration. "Write ... what ... I say."

I roll the tray table toward me and turn over the hospital menu. Then I pick up the forest green fine point, felt-tipped pen, and write as he talks.

1. Neon's parents love her.
2. Neon's parents are not mean.
3. No one's acting weird about Neon's broken wrist.
4. Neon isn't acting sick. Except for when she's being a hypochondriac.

"I'm not a hypochondriac!" I say.

Bobby ignores me. He keeps talking, faster and faster.

5. Rainbow is tired a lot.
6. Rainbow is twelve years old.
7. Twelve is old for a Lab mutt.

"Is that all?" I ask after he's quiet for a while.

"Add them up." His voice keeps rising and his hand starts with the one, two, three, four, five twisty finger thing in the air.

"Seven things. There's nothing to add."

"Read them," he says.

"I did," I say impatiently, "when I wrote them."

Bobby shifts his eyes. They meet mine for what must be the shortest measurable amount of time in the universe. Then they land on the menu in my hand. He stares through it like he's doing a menu mind meld or something. "Read. Them."

My stomach gets it before my brain does. It spins and flips until it's inside-out.

I don't have to read the list.

Because I already know.

"You're not dying," says Bobby.

A volcano of confusion explodes inside my chest.

No.

No. No. No.

My eyes begin to sting.

I do not cry in front of other people.

And I'm not about to cry in front of Bobby.

"I have to go."

I have to run. I have to run run run, run run run run run.

I stand and push off but lose my balance and crash into the railing at the end of Bobby's bed.

"I said you aren't dying," Bobby says, as I steady myself.

"Rainbow, c'mon." I nudge her off the bed, supporting her broken leg as she flops into the wagon.

She looks at me with Worry Face, then at Bobby, then at me again.

"Neeeeon." Bobby starts twisting his fingers again. One two three four five. One two three four five. "Why ... why aren't you ... happy?"

I don't answer as I hurry into the hall, bang the elevator button, and race inside. I hit Door Close and jerk the wagon in next to me. When we reach the lobby, I hurtle out and run home as fast as a person with a broken wrist pulling a red wagon with a fifty-five pound Rainbow can go.

I barrel across our lawn, the wagon bumping over dirt and grass. Crashing open the door, I tip the wagon to ease Rainbow out and clamber up the stairs to my bedroom. Dragging her broken leg, Rainbow trails behind me, clomping up the stairs one by one. We go into my room, and I slam the door closed.

My wrist is throbbing, and my chest begins to heave. I try to stop the sobs before they start, but it's no use. I help Rainbow climb on the bed next to me, curl myself around her, and bury my face in her bristly-soft black fur. She licks the tears from my salty cheeks. And blinks. One long dog blink that says everything will be okay.

I look into her warm brown eyes. Her warm, brown, never-ending pools of love that comfort me the way she always does.

But I'm the one who has to do the comforting now. Because I'm not dying.

Rainbow — my Rainbow — is.

Neon's Bedroom, Thursday, 5:30 p.m.

"Neon?" Mom knocks on my bedroom door. "Are you okay?"

"Yes," I say, but it comes out, "ya-uh ..." sniffle, sniffle, "... shshsh."

Mom opens my door slowly and sits on the bed next to Rainbow. "You must be exhausted from your first day back at school. You haven't budged since I got home from work."

I suck in my breath, but I can't stop the tears burning down my cheeks. Or the words tumbling out of my mouth.

When I finally finish talking, when I've told Mom everything, she's quiet. She stops petting Rainbow and clasps her hands together so tightly the tips of her fingers turn red and her knuckles turn white. Tears are streaming down her face, too, as she looks at me with an expression that makes my heart hurt before she says a word.

"Neon, sweetheart," she says. Her eyes still on mine, she holds me in her arms. I feel her tears against my wet cheek. "There's something I have to tell you."

Neon's Bedroom, Thursday, 6:00 p.m.

Two weeks, one day, eleven hours of thinking I was dying.

Two weeks, one day, eleven hours of confusion and anger and hurt.

22,260 minutes.

1,335,600 seconds.

And all because I thought my parents didn't care enough — didn't love me enough — to tell me.

Mom hugs me so close I see a tiny coffee stain on her buttercup yellow collar and smell the Freesia in her hair from her favorite shampoo—the organic one we buy her for special occasions because she says it's too extravagant. She's murmuring, over and over, "It's okay. It's okay."

"It's not. It's not okay," I shout, throwing her arms off me. "I thought I was dying, and you wouldn't tell me. I was so scared and confused and mad at you. And then today, Bobby said Rainbow's the one who's dying. And," a loud, Amber-like snort shoots from my nose and throat at the same time, "and now you tell me it's Mrs. Valentine who's been dying all along."

"Neon, honey." Her voice breaking, she wraps her arms around me again. "I'm sorry. I'm so sorry."

My ears are stuffed so full they're about to pop. Mom is stroking my hair, but she's not talking. And not making me talk.

I pull away to look at her. "How can she be dying when she hasn't even been in the hospital?"

"She has been. She's home now."

"I asked for a Miracle, but not this kind of Miracle. Not to trade Mrs. Valentine for me."

"Neon, that's not how—"

"Why isn't she still in the hospital if she's ... if she's ..."

"She wanted to be home, honey. Hospice is with her for several hours every day. Daddy and I and a few of her other close friends are taking turns sitting with her, too, so she's never alone."

"Hospice?"

"Like we used for Grandma. Do you remember?"

I shake my head.

"You were only three. Hospice is an organization that cares for people when they're dying."

Dying.

Mom says it like it's any old word.

My insides are exploding.

I want to scream at Mom again, but when I look at her, there are bags under her eyes and sadness deep inside them.

When did she start looking this way? Mom's eyes are always smiling, even when she's not. Who is this sad-eyed mom, and when did she sneak inside mine like some *Invasion of the Body Snatchers* imposter?

I thought I'd gotten better at this stuff. At noticing—really noticing—other people.

"You've always been so sweet to Mrs. Valentine," Mom interrupts my thoughts.

For the cookies, I want to yell.

But that's not true. I know it's not.

"Did Dad really help clean out her attic on Sunday?" I interrupt, my voice rising. "Is it even true?"

"Of course it's true. Last time Mrs. Valentine was in the hospital, she asked him to give her a hand with a few things in the house. She's had good days and bad days, but she's known for a while that her health was getting worse. She needed some time before she told other people."

"She told you and Dad." I turn away so Mom doesn't see the hurt I feel in my whole body. "Why didn't she tell me?"

Mom waits for a moment, then quietly says, "Why didn't you tell the people you love most that you thought you were going to die?"

I'm not sure if I know the answer. Not all of it, anyway.

"She'd like you to visit, to have a chance to talk—but only if you're up to it."

I want to go, but to see her now ....

I'm hit with a rush of memories, of Mrs. Valentine playing hide and seek with me when I was little, of the treats that miraculously appeared, of how interested she's always been in everything I do.

Always.

And of the good deeds I promised I'd do when I thought I was dying just hours ago.

I love Mrs. Valentine. And if I were dying—if I were really dying—I'd want her to visit me.

Mom and I walk to Mrs. Valentine's house. I ring the doorbell, and a woman about Mom's age opens the door.

"Hi, Rebecca," she says to Mom. "Mrs. Valentine will be glad to see you."

"Thank you, Keisha. I'll be by after dinner," Mom says, "but it's Neon who would like to visit now. Neon, this is Ms. LaGrange, Mrs. Valentine's nurse."

She doesn't look like a nurse in her black slacks and sleeveless red top.

"I'm so glad to meet you, Neon. Come on in." Ms. LaGrange motions with her arm. "Mrs. Valentine has told me so much about you."

"All set?" Mom whispers, giving me a hug.

I nod, but I'm not sure I can go through with this, after all. As Mom starts down Mrs. Valentine's front walk, I want to leave with her, but my feet don't move.

I mean, I can't move them at all. Not to leave, not to go inside. Like the first time in the cafeteria when I decided to sit with Bobby as a good deed—back when he was still Weird Bobby—and my feet froze when I wanted to change my mind.

Ms. LaGrange takes a step toward me, concern radiating from her hazel-brown eyes. "Are you okay?"

No, I think. I'm not okay. I'll never be okay without Mrs. Valentine. But I nod before I know I'm doing it, and somehow, I'm following Ms. LaGrange upstairs to Mrs. Valentine's room. Ms. LaGrange taps lightly and opens the bedroom door. She places her hand on my shoulder for a few seconds, then turns around and starts back down the stairs.

I've never seen Mrs. Valentine lying in bed before. She looks so small, leaning against a pile of pillows. Her twin bed is cranked into a sitting position. I wonder if she's always had a bed like that, or just since she's been sick. A white cotton blanket with tiny lavender flowers embroidered along the satin border covers her all the way up past her shoulders.

Her eyes are closed. I'm not sure if she's asleep or awake. It's only been a little over a week since I last saw her, but she doesn't look like I thought she would.

That's not quite right. I haven't had time to picture how she would look. I had kind of a vague idea, I guess, that she'd look more skeleton-like. More zombie-like.

More ... dead.

She looks like herself, except her curly gray hair isn't as perfect as usual. And her face looks tired. And thinner. Much thinner.

It couldn't have changed so much in such a short time.

But I didn't notice. Just like I didn't notice the sadness in Mom's eyes.

I look around the bedroom. The walls are eggshell blue with long, sheer curtains at the windows. A wedding photo in an antique silver frame like Mom and Dad's is on her dresser. I look at the framed photos of people I don't know lining the wall opposite the bed, then stop short.

The photo in the center, the biggest one, is of us, from about five years ago at the lake. I'm sitting on the sand next to the Dweeb, and Rainbow is lying next to me with her head in my lap. And sitting on the picnic bench behind us is Mrs. Valentine. It was the one and only time Mom and Dad convinced her to come to the lake. She only visited for the day because she said while there was no one in the whole world she wanted to be with more than us, she was more of an indoor plumbing kind of gal.

As I hold back the tears burning the corners of my eyes, Mrs. Valentine calls with a voice that sounds as wobbly as I feel.

"Neon." She pats the side of the bed. "Come. Sit."

"Is this okay?" I sit as close to the edge as I can, so I don't bump or bounce her.

She nods. "How's the wrist?"

"Not too bad," I say.

But I don't want to talk about my wrist. I'm not sure what I want to talk about. Except it should be about Mrs. Valentine. Not about me.

She smiles. It's a different smile, smaller and sadder than I'm used to, but filled with love, all the same.

"I've given some things to your mother," she says, "for you and Jonathan, but I have something I want to give you myself."

She twists and reaches to the other side of the bed, then sighs. "Neon, dear, could you grab that?" She points to her nightstand. "Behind the pitcher."

I see a blurry outline through the water in the clear plastic pitcher.

The heart-shaped Russell Stover Valentine's wishing box.

I walk over to pick it up. Then I hold it out to her.

She shakes her head. "You do the honors."

I place the box on my lap, but I don't open it. I look at Mrs. Valentine. "I only have one wish."

I circle my fingers around her hand. It feels as delicate as the wing of the baby sparrow Genna and I found in the garden last spring. I don't let go as the tears I can't hold back any longer escape and spill down my cheeks. Tears in front of someone else — not counting Rainbow; I'm allowed to cry in front of Rainbow — for the second time today.

Mrs. Valentine notches her thumb around my mine. "I've filled it with so many wishes, there might even be some for your own children one day," she says. "And let that sweet little brother of yours make a wish now and then when he needs some cheering up. Some of those wishes just may come true."

I'm wondering if she's told anyone else about the box when she starts coughing. A hacking cough that sounds as if it could shatter someone as thin and fragile as Mrs. Valentine into a million tiny pieces.

I pour water from the plastic pitcher into the cup on her nightstand and hold it out to her. As Mrs. Valentine takes the cup, her hands shake, so I lift it to her lips.

After a few moments, she squeezes my hand. I'm too afraid I'll hurt her if I squeeze back.

"Neon, dear," she begins, looking hard at me. "I've had a good life. And you, my darling girl, have been one of my greatest joys."

She tilts her head toward the box.

I rest my cast against it as I take off the soft, velvet lid. Each shiny gold compartment is filled with a nut- or cream- or toffee-filled chocolate. And piled on top of each chocolate are silver, red, and pink origami hearts.

For my dear Neon. With all my love. Your friend, Mrs. Isabelle Valentine is written in shaky, silver lettering on the pink origami heart in the center of the box.

Isabelle. Mrs. Valentine is Isabelle. Even my parents call her Mrs. Valentine.

Tears are streaming down my cheeks again. But this time, I don't care.

I want to ask if Mr. Valentine called her Isabelle, then I hear Bobby's voice in my head.

Stupid question, Neeeeon.

Stupid question.

CHAPTER FOURTEEN

Wednesday, Late Afternoon, Two Weeks Later

Rainbow and I are pretending to play Frisbee in our side yard. What we're actually doing is spying on the movers as they try to maneuver a table down the ramp from the truck to the sidewalk in front of Mrs. Valentine's house.

The movers are here because a new family is moving into Mrs. Valentine's house today. They have a girl a year younger than me and a boy the Dweeb's age.

Mom said, "How nice that you'll have a friend about your age next door."

I said, "I don't need a friend my age. I need Mrs. Valentine."

Then Mom told me that Mrs. Valentine sold her house to this unwanted family before she died so there wouldn't be any glitches during probate.

"What's probate?" I asked, even though I was trying not to care.

"Probate," Mom said, "is when the court makes sure everything is on the up and up so Mrs. Valentine's stuff goes to the people and places she left it to in her Will."

Apparently, this probate thing can drag on and on. Mrs. Valentine thought it would be too depressing for her neighbors if her house stood empty during all that dragging.

Then Mom gave me a look and said, "Neon, she didn't mean all the neighbors. She meant you. She picked this family for you — and Jonathan."

I held my stomach to try to squish away the emotions churning inside, but I didn't want to hide my tears for Mrs. Valentine from Mom. Not anymore. Because I never know when the tears will come. And because the only thing that helps when they do are Mom's arms around me.

The moving men are huge. The table is humongous. It's also

the ugliest thing I've ever seen. The top is a thick, wood slab in the grossest shade of diarrhea brown. The legs are big and fat with oversized wooden claws at the bottom. It won't fit inside the gate, so the moving men hoist it over the fence and into Mrs. Valentine's front yard.

Mrs. Valentine had all those cheerful new things so her house wouldn't feel like an old lady house. Our uninvited new neighbors are a whole lot younger, and all they have is horrible, old, moldy furniture that old people would hate.

At least Mrs. Valentine would hate it.

I wish they would put all that horrible stuff back in the horrible truck and go back to wherever they're moving from so I could forget about all of it.

Especially about the day Bobby told me it was Rainbow who was going to die. Because that was the day Mrs. Valentine went to the hospital for the last time.

I never knew Mrs. Valentine had been in the hospital a first time. Or a second.

And I never thought to check on her later if she wasn't home when I went over. I always went on my way, to school or cheerleading practice or orchestra. Even before a sleepover, I never bothered to see if she was okay.

Mrs. Valentine showed me over and over how much she loved me. I hope, somehow, she knows how much I loved her, too.

I'm grateful—trying to be grateful—that Mrs. Valentine was my neighbor for my whole life until now. I want her to still be here. And she's not.

But what I mostly feel is sad. So sad she's gone.

And guilty. Full-body-ache guilty.

Because it's all my fault.

My wish came true and in exchange Mrs. Valentine had to die.

Not everyone who is sick dies. Not everyone who is sick has someone making wishes—other wishes—that end up making them die instead.

"Neon?"

A voice interrupts my thoughts. Genna's voice. I turn toward her like I have for my whole life. Then I freeze.

"Neon." She touches my arm and walks around to face me.

"You're back," I say without looking at her. Right after school was out, Genna's family went to visit her grandma in California.

"How're you feeling?" She looks at my cast. "Does it hurt?"

I shake my head. "Not anymore."

"I'm sorry," she says, after a pause.

"I know."

I do. Mom told me that Genna and Maddie said they were sorry when they brought over Amber's silver sandals for the Snowflake Dance. Genna texted from California and kept texting to say she was sorry about Mrs. Valentine, too. She finally stopped when I never answered.

It's not that I'm mad at Genna anymore. I just don't know—I don't even know what it is I don't know—except that everything between us feels wrong. It feels like we're slipping on ice when everything between us used to be so easy.

"I'm really sorry about Mrs. Valentine. She loved you a lot."

"Thank you," I say. I feel like Bobby as I focus on an especially pretty pink climbing rose on Mrs. Valentine's white picket fence.

"And," Genna bites her lip, but the tears she's trying to stop fill her eyes anyway, "I'm grateful to Weird Bobby."

"Bobby," I say.

"Huh?"

"Call him Bobby," I say.

The flicker in her chocolate eyes tells me that her computer brain gets why.

"I'm so grateful to Bobby for saving my best friend's life," she says.

I don't answer. Genna tries to have heart-to-soul talks like this sometimes, but I never want to. This talk is already making me itch.

"Neez, I totally get that you're mad, and that I hurt your feelings. But you ditched us. We didn't know why. I didn't know why."

"I didn't ditch you."

"You did. I asked why you weren't sitting with Maddie and Amber and me at lunch. You wouldn't tell me. You didn't even text or call to say you were coming home with your family from the lake. And for all that time, you were acting ... different. All I know is if I ever thought I was dying, you'd be the first person I'd tell."

I look up, stunned.

"Bobby told Knuckles. Knuckles told Jessie. Jessie told Amber and—"

I nod. "Genna, I'm sorry." I'm not sure where those words came from, but as I say them, I realize they're true. "I couldn't tell. I ... couldn't. Every time I tried to say that I was dying out loud, I—"

"Yes. You could." Genna is trying to be very still, but the corners of her mouth are hovering between angry and sad. "You did. You told Bobby."

"That was before he was a person. Before he was ... my friend." I pause, then add, "When he was only a good deed."

Genna doesn't say anything. I'm not sure if she knows about the good deeds. I'm not sure if I'll tell her. Maybe someday, when we're really old.

Or maybe next week.

"Valentine! Come back!" a boy's voice wails.

Valentine? My heart lurches.

A gray and white kitten leaps and scampers across the lawn, her tiny, strong legs pushing off with every step.

I bend and scoop her into my right hand before she rushes past us to the street. Her fur is soft against my skin, but she's squirming to escape my grasp.

"Hey, kitty," I say.

She looks at me with the sweetest bluish-gold eyes. She holds my gaze for a long time. Then her squirming stops. She begins purring and settles into my arms.

Genna reaches over to pet her. "She's adorable."

"That's Valentine," the boy says, running up to us. "I'm Liam."

"Valentine?" I frown.

"For the lady who went to Heaven. Mommy says she was really something special. We're moving into her house."

Tears.

I take a deep breath.

No tears. No tears. No tears.

They stop. From my right eye. The tears from my left eye trickle down my cheek, but Liam doesn't see them. I'm not as sure about Genna.

"Do you live there?" He points to my house and looks at Genna and me.

"I do."

"You're Neon, right?" he continues.

I nod. "And this is Genna."

He squints at Genna, and she smiles.

"Hey, how do you know my name?" I ask.

"Neon's a funny name. Mrs. Valentine told my parents that Neon and her brother Jonathan, whose nickname's J.B. and who's my age, live next door. You don't look my age. I wasn't sure if you look like a Neon because I've never met one before."

I hand Valentine back to him.

"How old is she?" Genna asks.

He scrunches his face at the watch that's too big for his wrist. "Twelve weeks, four days, five hours, and seventeen and a half minutes."

"Okay, then," I say. "Well, see you around."

He doesn't turn to go. He's looking at me the way the Dweeb does when he's hoping.

"What?" I ask.

He looks down, suddenly shy. "Nothing."

The moving men are carrying an antique couch. It's even uglier than the table, with its puke orange upholstery and more of that same diarrhea-colored wood.

I feel someone looking at me and glance in Genna and Rainbow's direction.

There are two pairs of brown eyes sending laser beam signals in my direction. Genna raises an eyebrow. Rainbow's ear flops down. They each give me the "C'mon, Neon" look.

For Pete's sake. It's not like I have to do good deeds anymore.

"Are you hungry?" The words come out of my mouth before I know I've thought them. But he's probably starving. They've been moving in all day.

"Kind of." Liam shrugs.

"Me, too," says Genna.

"Follow me." I give Genna a tiny nod as she takes his hand. "You're going to love my mom's banana bread."

Rainbow stops and gives me a look I've never seen before.

I give her a look she's never seen before right back.

She doesn't flinch.

I sigh.

I know what she wants me to do.

"So long as you're here," I say to Liam, "you might as well meet my brother."

I look at Rainbow.

She turns and hobbles up the three steps to our back porch, nudges open the screen door, and waits. I walk past her into the kitchen. Genna follows me, and Liam, with Valentine in his arms, follows Genna.

When we're all snug inside, Rainbow blinks her warm brown eyes, curves her mouth, and smiles.

Her great big filled-with-love Rainbow smile.

I toss a bite of banana bread into the silver dog food bowl from Mrs. Valentine's house. Dragging her broken leg, Rainbow pads over.

And the screen door closes behind her.

About the Author

Meira Rosenberg began *28 Days of Neon*, a New Voices in Children's Literature: Tassy Walden Awards finalist, while vacationing with her family at their cabin in Maine. Her novel, *Indiana Bamboo*, won the Tennessee Mountain Writers Excalibur Award for a first-time novelist and First Prize in the category of Children's Book-Fiction in the Connecticut Press Club Awards.

She received her MFA in Creative Writing from Manhattanville College and has taught English and Writing at the University of Connecticut and Connecticut State Community College. She is also a lawyer and a former Literary Trustee of the Lorraine Hansberry Properties Trust. Meira loves visiting schools, bookstores, and libraries, and especially enjoys the wonderful imaginations of her students in creative writing workshops.

She and her husband have three children who are now young adults, and who, while growing up, had dogs, cats, guinea pigs, hamsters, goldfish, hermit crabs, and the occasional garter snake who was banished to a terrarium on the front porch. Now they live with one rambunctious pup who is as wise as Rainbow and who loves to dance.

Learn more at www.MeiraRosenberg.com